Summer Song

Summer
Song

Susan Rowan Masters

Clarion Books/New York

*For support and encouragement, special thanks
to my editor, Nina Ignatowicz.*

Clarion Books
a Houghton Mifflin Company imprint
215 Park Avenue South, New York, NY 10003
Text copyright © 1995 by Susan Rowan Masters

Printed in the USA.
Type is 12.5 Meridien.
Book design by Carol Goldenberg.

Library of Congress Cataloging-in-Publication Data
Masters, Susan Rowan.
Summer song / by Susan Rowan Masters.
p.   cm.
Summary: Etta May struggles to face her grandfather's
inevitable death and to overcome her hostility toward the
mother who abandoned her when she was a baby.
ISBN 0-395-71127-4
[1. Grandfathers—Fiction.   2. Mothers and daughters—Fiction.
3. Death—Fiction.]   I. Title.
PZ7.M423932Su   1995
[Fic]—dc20   94-43684
                            CIP
                            AC
BP   10   9   8   7   6   5   4   3   2   1

This is for my sister,
Deanie LaPlante Blank—
with admiration
with love

Chapter One

I've got this skirt. It's navy polyester and it sucks up all the lint and dust within a six-block radius. All I have to do is put it on and *whoosh*, I'm standing there in this dust rag. I'm like that skirt. I suck up every speck of disaster that's lying in wait.

That morning, while I was cooking up some scrambled eggs, I couldn't help but eye Ma's letter over by the fridge. It was addressed to my grandpa Gent. I'd been dying to take a peek at what was inside, but I didn't dare in front of Gent. He'd been awful quiet since it came. Seeing him like that gave me a bad feeling, like a whole new batch of disasters were sitting right there on the counter ready to pounce.

"Git off my property, you scalawag!" shouted Gent.

I turned around to see what was happening. We lived in this trailer, Gent and me, so I could see him in the living room from where I stood. He had a big ol' stuffed rocker plunked smack next to the front window, where he spent most of his time. That was so he could see what was going on with all the neighbors. 'Course, he'd never have admitted to it. Anyway, Gent was out of his chair waving his arms and banging on the window.

I knew it had to be the next-door neighbor's mongrel either peeing on our trailer or digging around Gent's roses. Zip seemed to prefer Summer Song, Gent's favorite rosebush, to anything else. Gent's roses lined the place, fanning out to the driveway on either side. Starting in late spring, our tiny piece of land changed like Cinderella did when the fairy godmother waved her magic wand. After my grandma Manny died, Gent didn't work on the roses as much, though, mostly just doing some hoeing and shooing ol' Zip away.

"I'll go scare him off with a stone." I hoped that would calm Gent before he got worked up any more and started wheezing.

"*Scat!*" Gent shouted, jabbing both hands in the air. He lost his balance and began to fall toward the window.

I dropped the spatula and plowed into him like a star linebacker. The collision sent Gent flying backward into the rocker with so much force that it fell over too. He ended up with his head touching the floor and his feet pointing up at the ceiling.

"Gent, are you okay?" I asked, trying to keep my voice from trembling. I got down on my hands and knees and clasped the back of his chair. "*Speak to me,*" I begged.

He sat completely still. Deep-set eyes under wiry brows stared back, unblinking.

Oh, Lord, could somebody die with their eyes wide open? I panicked. Leaning over his left ear, I screamed, "*Gent!*"

He blinked. "I ain't deaf, Etta May. And I ain't dead yet, neither."

"You trying to give me a heart condition?" I asked.

Gent was always saying that to me. I thought it might make him chuckle a little so he'd forget it was me who accidentally pushed him a bit too hard into his chair. But I knew why he wouldn't answer till he had to—so he could scare the wits out of me. That's Gent, always giving back just enough so you know not to do it again.

"You look kinda funny with your feet pointing straight up to heaven like that." This time I heard him chuckle. Then before he could say anything, I grabbed the back of the chair and shoved.

"Stop!" demanded Gent. "I don't need no more of your help!"

I kept pushing. "It's no bother, Gent, honest," I grunted.

"I can get up my—" Before he could finish, I gave the chair one last big heave and pushed it back into the upright position. Gent, sitting stiff as the Lincoln Memorial statue, stared out the window in stony silence. Finally, he muttered, "That dog's gonna rot out the place."

"We'll buy some more mothballs to put out there," I said, going back to the stove and turning it off. The eggs were hard and rubbery. "That should keep ol' Zip away." But I kept quiet about the place rotting out because it already was in pretty bad shape. Dog pee wasn't going to make a bit of difference.

"You ain't throwing away those eggs," Gent called with his back to me.

How does Gent always know when I'm about to throw away food? I thought, staring at the pan angled over the garbage bin. I threw it back on the stove with a bang. "I should've let you fall and watched you lay on the hard floor while I ate my nice soft eggs," I muttered. Even though I sounded mad, I didn't mean it.

Gent's my only real family. I had a ma all right, but she was way out in Pittsburgh, Pennsylvania. That's not saying a whole lot. I'd seen her all of nine times, and that includes the day I was born.

I guess you could say my first disaster was getting born to a ma who didn't want me.

She'd call and send money every so often, and sometimes act like she wanted me to live with her. But she'd say she had to get a job that paid enough so she could afford a decent place to bring up a kid. That doesn't change the fact she dumped me here and then took off. I guess taking care of a squalling baby wasn't part of her plans. I don't mean it like it might sound. After all, I was lucky to have Gent and Manny take me in.

The last time I'd seen Ma was seven months ago. She drove up in a beat-up Plymouth and stayed a couple of weeks to help out before Manny died. I couldn't figure out why she had come, until I decided it was probably guilt on her part for all the years she wasn't around.

Gent was awful quiet while Ma was here, moping around the trailer and not saying much to anybody, including Ma. Not even after the funeral, when everybody was leaving the cemetery and two men were getting ready to lower Manny's casket down the hole. We had got back into the shiny black funeral car and Ma reached over to me. "Come here, baby," she whispered when she saw me bawling my eyes out. "Come to your mama."

But I didn't want anyone getting hold of me just

then and pawing me. Especially Ma. All I wanted was Manny's soothing arms around me like before. So I scrunched up tight against the door. The handle stuck into my side like a cold, hard thorn.

Gent looked over at me and, from the sadness in his eyes, I knew he was thinking about Manny too. So I reached across Ma and put my hand into his. Bony and veined as it was, it felt comforting.

Ma opened up her shoulder bag and took out a cigarette. She sat there puffing on it and staring ahead. Nobody said anything. Not even after the limo dropped us off at the funeral home, where we climbed into Ma's Plymouth and she drove us the rest of the way home.

The next morning Ma packed up and left.

I didn't mean for her to leave and never come back. I should've gone to her then and asked her to stay; but I guess I didn't because of all the hurting I had inside.

When I was little I used to dream about her.

Ma, dressed all fancy, would pull up in one of those big, classy cars. She'd step out smiling and happy and tell us she was taking us—Gent, Manny, and me—back to Pittsburgh with her. Next thing Ma would be driving us slowly up a long curvy driveway and stopping in front of a white house with columns that reached clear to the sky. "From now on you're living here with me," she'd say. In my dream her face was beautiful, like it is in the faded color picture on Manny's bureau.

"We're doing fine without her," I muttered, forcing her out of my thoughts. Then I glanced at the clock over the stove. I was running late. Any second, Mrs. Traub would be hauling up in the school bus and, if I wasn't out by the main road pronto, she'd lay on the horn before taking off.

I had to get to school or I'd end up in trouble again. So I scrambled to my room at the back of the trailer to get my books.

HOOOONNNNK!

Whirling, I ran out the door and to the end of our road just as the bus was pulling away. From the engine's high whir, I could tell Mrs. Traub had really stepped on it. Black smoke belched from the exhaust pipe. Throwing down my books, I shook my fists at the back of the bus and hoped ol' pie face was looking out her rearview mirror.

Chapter Two

I went back inside. Gent was on his knees, poking his head into the cabinet below the kitchen sink. There was a lot of banging of pipes and muttering going on.

"*Gent,*" I yelled over the noise. "You have to drive me to school."

"Where'd I put that wrench?" he asked, his voice gravelly.

"Didn't you hear me? I missed the bus. You have to take me to school *now.*" Even though I was glad to see him beginning to take an interest in the place again, I didn't want to be late.

Gent turned toward me, clanking his head on a pipe. He began rubbing the sore spot and muttering a few cuss words that would have sent our neighbor, the Carrot Lady, flying into her trailer if she'd been within earshot. Gripping the edge of the sink and wheezing from the effort, Gent slowly pulled himself to his feet.

All the way to school he kept wheezing. It was getting worse, I thought, watching his thin shoulders. They worked up and down as if a rock was attached to each one and he was trying his darnedest to haul those rocks up with every breath.

"It's been a while since you've seen Doc Kelsy. Maybe you should go," I said. When it came to doctors and hospitals, Gent had his own ideas.

After Manny died, Gent made me promise on a solemn oath that I would never let anybody take him to the hospital. "When the time comes, Etta May," he had said, "you let me die in peace and quiet in my own bed. Like the good Lord intended." He had it in his head that Manny would have lived longer—or at least more peacefully—if she hadn't gone to the hospital where the doctors could get their hands on her.

Maybe Gent was right, I thought, remembering Manny hooked up to a bunch of machines, looking so shriveled and helpless. Still, I worried for him. And for me too.

"You got doctor on the brain?" he asked as we pulled up to the school's side entrance. "I already told you, Etta May, there's nothin' more Doc can do for my emphysema." It wasn't like he said it mean. And I knew he wasn't mad at me either, because he held his face out so I could give him a peck on the cheek.

But I knew I wasn't to bring up the subject again.

As the pickup drove off, I heard the tailpipe dragging. Oh, Lord, I thought, one more thing that needs fixing.

I was glad the outside of the building was deserted, even though it meant the tardy bell had probably rung. At least nobody saw me get out of our rust bucket, I thought, hurrying inside and up the stairs to room 207. If I was lucky, Mr. Fisher, my homeroom teacher, would probably have his back to the door and I could slip inside. I held my ear to the closed door. But all I heard was my heavy breathing.

That was when I remembered Mr. Fisher telling us yesterday we were to be weighed and measured first thing this morning.

Downstairs, I quietly opened the door to the gym and tiptoed inside. Everybody was either sitting on the floor or leaning against the back wall. I slid in beside Quentin Oaks. "Where you been?" he whispered. "I hung around your place until the bus came this morning."

Before I could answer, Mr. Fisher called from the front, "Did you bring your attendance card, Etta May?"

I shook my head.

"We're almost done here. You might just as well

come up now and get weighed and measured," he added, frowning at me. Anybody late was supposed to go to the office first and ask the secretary for their attendance card and bring it to Mr. Fisher. Then they had to take it back again to the office. I didn't see why the secretary couldn't mark it herself.

"Sixty-two inches," the nurse called to Mr. Fisher, who wrote it into my health record.

I figured in my head that I was two inches over five feet. Taller than Ma was at my age, I recalled, stepping up on the scale. I knew that because Manny had marked out Ma's height on the inside cover of the Bible every year up to Ma's fourteenth birthday. She always called Ma her miracle child because at forty-three she had never been pregnant, then along came Ma. And I was her miracle grandchild. But I figured getting stuck with a kid after all those years was no miracle. Just a whole lot of work.

The nurse wrinkled her brow. "Ninety-seven," she called to Mr. Fisher. Then quietly to me, she added, "You need to put on more weight, Etta May. Eat all the butter and ice cream you want."

Butter and ice cream? Weren't those things supposed to be bad for you? But it didn't matter none. Gent and I hardly ever had enough money left over to buy real butter, let alone ice cream. Besides, ninety-seven pounds was nothing to worry over, not like Gent's wheezing spells or that letter from Ma.

All day long I thought about that letter. I could barely keep my mind on mixed fractions and President Lincoln and the Civil War. When the bell finally rang at the end of seventh period I was extra glad to get on home so I could try to see what it said.

"Wait up," called Quentin, hurrying up the bus steps and over to me. He plunked himself down on the seat beside me. "Why you been ignoring me?"

"I have not!" I shot back.

"Don't have to get mad, Etta May," he said, his shoulders slumping. "How come you didn't come out when I called for you this morning?"

"I wasn't ignoring you, Quentin. I was in the back getting my books because I was running late, so I couldn't have heard you no matter what. Besides, I got lots of things on my mind."

Quentin took out a tissue and blew his nose. "What kind of things?" he asked, stuffing the tissue back into his pocket.

"You know, like Gent not going to see Doc Kelsy about his spells anymore. This morning he could hardly catch his breath."

Quentin slowly shook his head. He would never

say something like "Your grandpa's going to be okay" just to make me feel better, without knowing it was the honest-to-God truth. So he said nothing. But I knew he understood.

Quentin lived in the same trailer court as me. Sunshine Pines, it was called. There was nothing sunshiny about the place, just a bunch of old trailers lined up every twenty feet or so and a few scrappy-looking pine trees.

We'd known each other a long time, Quentin and me. Ever since we were little we'd been friends. Even back then he was tall and all angles so his clothes never quite fit. Some of the kids at Liberty Junior High called Quentin a retard or Simple Simon behind his back because he spent part of the day in a special class. But he was neither, just slow about some things. I didn't care what the other kids said, because Quentin had qualities that made me forget the rough edges. Like his singing. He had a sweet voice and could make up words to his own country-western songs in no time. And Quentin was the most honest person I knew, and hardly ever ill-tempered like me. Sometimes he could be too honest, though, to the point where he told people too much.

The bus rolled to a stop by the rickety Sunshine Pines sign. The doors closed behind us with a rush of air and Quentin and I took off down the road.

"It's gonna rain," he said, turning his face to the sky.

"Look." I nodded in the direction of the trailer beside ours. "I'll bet the Carrot Lady came out just to snoop on us."

Mrs. Morales touched a hand to her reddish-orange hair and smoothed back a curl. "Hello there, Etta May, Quentin." After Manny died, she'd come over to our place every so often with one excuse or another to nose around. Like we couldn't get along without her help. Gent never seemed to mind, but I did.

I nodded in her direction and kept walking. But Quentin brightened up with a big smile and a wave.

"Your grandpa's been inside all day," she called. "On a nice spring day like this I expected to see him working around his roses. I hope he's not ailing."

"There's nothing wrong with Gent. He's been fixing up some things inside, that's all." Though I wouldn't tell her, Quentin knew I was worried over Gent spending most of his time staring out the front window or watching game shows on TV since Manny died.

Quentin turned to me and started to open his mouth when I gave him a shush-up look. What I'd told Mrs. Morales was partly the truth. Wasn't

Gent working on the kitchen plumbing that very morning?

"Well, I'm glad to hear it." Then she turned to Quentin and started in on him. "And how's your pa like his new job, Quentin?"

"He likes it fine, I guess, except for—"

"Quentin and me got to go now," I quickly added. Grabbing Quentin by his arm, I hauled him along. "Don't go shootin' off your mouth to people about your personal stuff," I said when we were out of earshot. "Especially people like the Carrot Lady, who don't care a whit about anybody except for what they can pass on in gossip."

"But she asked me. Why did you tell her your grandpa isn't ailing, when he is?"

"'Cause it's none of the old snoop's business. And if you want to know, you'd be a whole lot better off telling her as little as possible too. Unless you want your private business spread all over Chautauqua County."

"Maybe you're right, Etta May," said Quentin. Stopping in front of my place, he kicked a stone and watched the trail of dust move across the dirt road.

"You bet I'm right." Like I said, Quentin was honest all right, but he needed someone to watch out for his interests so he didn't get hurt any more than necessary. Three years ago his ma had run off with another man. One way or another, we were both missing our mothers. It was one of the things that made Quentin and me understand each other so well.

"Did you hear that?"

A distant roll of thunder sounded and rain began to fall in big droplets. "Oh, Lord," I cried, "I gotta go." I ran up the stoop, grabbing two pails on the landing. Inside, I put them in the kitchen where it was starting to drip.

Gent, lying flat out in his chair, was snoring up a thunderous storm of his own. Since I figured he wasn't about to wake up, I went back into the kitchen and picked up Ma's letter real quiet. I recognized the squiggly writing. It was sort of like mine, only harder to read; but then I suppose it's a whole lot easier to read something you've written yourself.

"Dear Pop," it began,

> You never say much over the phone, but I've had this feeling something was wrong. Maybe because you've been extra careful lately telling me that nothing *was* wrong. Anyway, that's why I phoned Doctor Kelsy's office earlier today.
>
> He said he called you, but you refused to come back for another appointment. Why didn't you tell me? I guess I'm not surprised,

since it's just like you not to tell me anything.
Does Etta May know?

Know what? I wondered, my face growing hot.
What did they both know that I didn't?

> I'm taking time off from work to drive
> down this weekend. No use trying to call me
> up to argue about it.

"Etta May?"
I looked up and saw Gent out of his chair, facing
me. "What do you and Ma know that I don't?" I
demanded. When he didn't answer, I threw down
the letter and ran out the door into the rain.

Chapter Three

My legs pumped as hard as I could make them go. Out past the main road, past the railroad tracks, and into the woods, where I finally stopped to catch my breath. I turned around then and saw Gent in the pickup driving slowly along the road.

Looking up between the branches at the angry sky, I let the cold rain run down my face and neck. I'm not going to cry, I thought, I'm not going to cry, *I'm not going to cry.* But the hot tears came anyway. Finally I went back to the main road, where the pickup crept along the shoulder toward me.

Gent pulled up and unlatched the passenger door. It swung open.

I didn't move. "You tell it to me straight, Gent," I said, wiping my sleeve across my face. "You tell it to me straight or I head right on into town and over to Doc Kelsy's."

I waited till he finally nodded before I climbed in beside him.

Gent started driving slowly toward home. "Even on a good day it'd take all of two hours to walk to town," he said. "Doc would be gone by the time you made it clear over to his place."

I put my hand on the door handle and moved closer like I was about to jump.

"Now, Etta May. You don't have to get worked up over nothin'."

"*Nothing!*" I yelled. "Lord, don't you think I got any sense? Any sense at all?"

Gent pulled off the road and cut the engine before slumping over the steering wheel. He was silent for a moment, his thin shoulders working up and down a couple of times. Then he looked over at me.

"I know you got plenty of sense, likely more'n me. But Doc won't tell you much, Etta May . . . just that he had me go for some tests awhile back and all they found was a shadow on one of my X rays." I could see he was having a hard time getting the words out. "Just a shadow," he repeated as if to himself, "and your ma makes a big to-do over it."

"What do you mean, awhile back? You haven't been to see Doc since . . . since just after Manny died." And then I knew why he hadn't gone back and why he hadn't told anybody either. Gent was scared. Scared of getting sent to the hospital like Manny and what might happen if he did.

I thought of Manny not being here anymore to put her arms around me and comfort me with her soft voice. I wanted her, needed her to tell me what to do.

*   *   *

Ma is stepping out of a brand-new Lincoln that stretches clear to the end of our driveway. She turns and begins floating toward me, her arms reaching out. "You and Pop are coming back with me," she says, her face shining, "back to Pittsburgh." But there is something strange in her smile, and while I'm trying real hard to figure out what it is, a bomb explodes.

The noise from Gent's alarm made me jump. The walls were so thin, almost like there was nothing but air between us. I could hear Gent breathing on the other side.

"Ma," I whispered, remembering my dream. Why would I start dreaming of her again? I wondered, shuffling into the bathroom. I closed her out of my thoughts.

By the time I finished getting washed and dressed for school, Gent was in the kitchen cooking up a pot of oatmeal. I wrinkled my nose at it. "I'll have some toast," I said, getting out a slice of bread and popping it into the toaster. But Gent went ahead and dished out two bowls anyway and set them on the table.

"Where's the third person?" I asked, smart-like, and looked around. "I don't see anybody."

Gent grunted.

I started feeling bad for giving him a hard time, so I put some brown sugar and milk in my bowl and ate a couple of spoonfuls.

"Etta May," I heard from outside our trailer. *"Etta May?"*

"Why don't that boy give a knock on the door instead of a holler like he does?" asked Gent.

I grabbed my books in one hand and the toast in the other and headed for the door. "Probably because of the time you got after him for banging on the door."

"Hmph."

I was almost out the door when Gent called, "Etta May?"

"Oh, yeah, I almost forgot," I said, taking four steps back and giving him a peck on his grizzly cheek.

Outside, Quentin was parked on the edge of our stoop, softly humming to himself.

"One of your new songs?" I asked. He got up and we started for the end of our road.

"Naw, just something I heard last night on TV."

Then Quentin, pretending he was picking on a guitar, began to sing.

I hooted and hollered and laughed so hard at the words I thought my sides would burst. "Who you wishing to chase 'round the room? Oh, I bet I know. It's Naomi, isn't it?" Puckering up my lips, I flung out my arms and began running around like I was chasing after Naomi. "Now you come back here and give your lover boy a big ol' kiss."

Quentin's ears flushed pink and he turned his back to me. "None of your business, Etta May."

I stopped and looked over at him staring down the long, curvy road. "Shoot, Quentin, I'm only having some fun." But I knew I was having fun at his expense and I didn't blame him none for not talking to me. Worrying over the shadow on Gent's X ray and wondering about Ma's coming back to do who-knows-what was getting to me. But that was no excuse for my orneriness.

Quentin never could stay silent for long. On the bus ride over to school he talked about the Hank Williams electric guitar that was sitting in the window of Westermyer's music store over at the mall. For the past month, Quentin had been riding his bike the five miles back and forth 'most every day just to eye it in the window. "Pa said I had to be sixteen and get a job first before I could even think about buying it. But I'll die if I have to wait that long."

"You want it pretty bad," I said and looked out the window before I spoke again. "My ma's driving down from Pittsburgh." The words came out so quiet Quentin barely heard me above the roar of the bus. "She'll be here tonight."

"How come you didn't tell me before now?" he asked.

"I only found out myself."

"Why is she coming this time?"

"I think she's worried Gent's getting sicker."

I remembered that after Manny's funeral Quentin told me, "Don't you go worrying over your grandpa too. Nothing's going happen to him, Etta May. But if it did, you always got me and Pa."

"At least you get to see her sometimes," he whispered now. Quentin had a sad, faraway look in his eyes, as though he were wishing it was his own ma who was coming back. He believed that problems had easy answers. Like, if she did choose to come home, everything could be put back right.

But I knew better.

Chapter Four

❧❧❧❧❧❧

Gent didn't seem to know what time Ma was coming, except that it would be late. He had shuffled off to his room, leaving orders to let him know when she got in.

A flash of headlights swept past the front window. I turned off "The Tonight Show" and went over to open the door. Instead of the beat-up Plymouth I remembered from seven months ago, a Volkswagen stood out front. Ma was getting out, dressed in jeans and a man's flannel shirt. I don't know what I expected; a big fancy car like the one in my dream, maybe?

She went to the backseat and pulled out a suitcase. "Etta May," she said, coming up the steps and through the door. "It can't be that long since I was here last, but I swear you've grown another foot." She put down the case and looked me over like she was considering the possibility of giving me a hug.

Just in case she got the wrong idea, I moved to the other side of the room, not far enough for my taste, but considering the size of the place I didn't have much choice. Ma made it sound like she came often, which was a downright lie.

I wasn't ready to wake Gent up, not until I got some straight answers from her first. "What did Doc tell you about Gent? He's got to have more than a shadow on an X ray for you to drive clear down from Pittsburgh. The only reason you'd come back is if somebody's dying."

"That's not true."

"Then why did you wait till Manny was about ready to die?" I demanded.

Ma fished around inside her purse for a cigarette. "They never told me anything until it was almost too late. Look, I've had a long day, and I don't need . . ." She went into the kitchen and picked up a saucer. "Let's not start by arguing," she said, taking a long drag on the cigarette and tapping the ashes into the saucer. "I'll tell you all I know, okay? I called Dr. Kelsy's office early last week because I suspected something was wrong. I don't know, intuition maybe. Anyway, I found out that when they did some tests on Pop six months ago they found something on his left lung. Since then he hasn't gone back."

"It could be nothing," I said. "That's what Gent says and he could be right, you know."

"Don't get your hopes up."

"That you, Claire?" called Gent from his bedroom. "Is everything all right?"

"Just fine, Pop," Ma answered, grinding the cigarette into the saucer before going down the hall into his room. I heard the muffled sound of their voices and was about to go to my room when Ma came back. "Kelsy's office got us in to see a specialist tomorrow," she said. "I haven't told Pop yet because it's not worth getting him upset over it tonight." Ma set her jaw in a way that reminded me of Gent when he was determined about something. "One way or another, Etta May, we'll get him to go, even if it takes knocking him out cold and dragging him there."

I couldn't stop myself from grinning at the thought of Ma and me trying to move the Rock of Gibraltar. "No one I know is more stubborn than Gent."

"Stubborn," she repeated, "yet sometimes too trusting."

I didn't know what she meant. It made me think of one long-ago visit when I was little. Ma had taken me aside and told me never to get into a car or go into somebody's house without my grandma or grandpa being there with me. I told her I already knew about that stuff, but she just stared hard at me and added, "*Even* if you know that person."

The thing I understood least of all was how she could act like she cared and then go off and leave her own flesh and blood.

Ma kicked off her shoes. "I'm so beat I can hardly hold my eyes open," she said, pulling Manny's afghan around her as she stretched out on the couch. Her eyes fluttered and she called my name so quietly I barely heard it. "Etta May, honey? How 'bout a goodnight kiss?"

Though I didn't want to, I did go over to her. She reached up and touched my face. Acting friendly didn't change one iota all those years she was never around, so I turned away and left her on the couch, alone.

As soon as I crawled into bed my thoughts turned to Manny. I guess it was Ma talking about taking Gent to the doctor. Last year, when Manny was so sick, taking her to the County Hospital in Liberty seemed like the right thing to do. But soon as the doctors started hooking her up to all those machines, she got worse. And all that praying Pastor Duncan did over her didn't help either, not in the way I wanted. "Sister Loomis is healed in the Lord's spirit," Pastor Duncan had told Gent and me the day before she died. "She's ready to meet her Maker."

"Can't you heal more than her spirit?" I cried.

"It's the Lord's will. You have to accept that, Etta May." I noticed Pastor Duncan's shoes polished to a crisp, shiny black. "Your grandmother has."

But I figured Manny knew she would never go home again, so she just gave up.

That wasn't going to happen to Gent. I'd see to it.

* * *

"I didn't come all this way just to look at you over a carton of milk, Pop," Ma said early the next morning as I wandered into the kitchen and sat at the counter. She moved aside the gallon container that Gent had plunked down in front of her.

"Anybody here ask you to come?" Gent answered. Just as Ma was about to say something, he slipped in, "You can stop getting all worked up, Claire, 'cause I've decided to go." Gent picked up his coffee mug and took a long sip as if he were having a quiet, restful morning.

Both Ma and I sat there with our mouths open.

It took him all of five seconds to go through the motions of enjoying his coffee before putting it back down. "Just to prove you and Doc wrong. Except for a few spells, there's nothin' wrong with me." He thumped his chest with his fist. "Heart's never been stronger."

Gent was like that when you least expected it. "Turns on a dime," Manny would say. "He'd drive any sane person crazy." But I figured it was his way of letting people know he was still calling the shots.

On the way into Liberty, Gent sat up front with Ma and pointed out the new landfill. "A dump, that's what I call it. When Mason Carter died, his wife ended up selling off part of their land to the county. Awful shame none of their boys took over the place."

Ma, with one hand on the wheel, started taking a cigarette out of her shoulder bag, and then thought better of it. "Do you know if Willie is still around?" she asked.

"Willie," Gent repeated with a chuckle. "Their youngest, wasn't he? The one who used to show up at our place all times of the day and sit outside, just waiting for you to come on out?"

Ma nodded.

"Last I heard he'd moved West."

I didn't know these people. It was strange to think about a time I wasn't part of. And I wondered, could Willie Carter be my daddy? Once I got up enough nerve to ask Manny about my pa— if she knew who he was, and such. Her mouth flattened into a line. "No need to go thinkin' about somebody who took off long ago, even before you was born." But for a long time afterward, I couldn't stop thinking about him. Did he know about me?

At the doctor's office, Ma and I sat in the waiting room while Gent was examined. When Ma was called in for a chat, I worried over what was being said. It seemed to take forever. When she finally returned without Gent, I demanded, "What's going on?"

"He needs some special tests." Ma took a deep breath. "That means two or three days over at the County Hospital."

"Hospital!" I screamed. "Nobody's taking Gent *anywhere* but home." I didn't care if people turned their heads to stare at us or not.

"Etta May," Ma said, looking at me square on, "I don't want any trouble. You hear me?" Her gray eyes narrowed and her mouth was set in a line that reminded me of Manny's when she didn't want any back talk. "After he's done filling out some papers, I'm taking him to the hospital. If you want, you can come along. Or you can stay right here and I'll pick you up on my way home." Then she turned and started toward the examining rooms.

After a minute or so, I got up and slowly followed. Two or three days, huh? Sure, I thought, I'll just bet that's all it'll be. On the way over to the hospital I didn't say another word to her, and she and Gent were quiet too.

We waited till Gent was settled in bed before we got ready to leave.

"It's only for a couple of days," I whispered in his ear and then kissed him on the cheek.

Gent took my hand and held on tight before finally letting go. "You keep an eye on Zip for me, Etta May, so he don't go digging around my roses." That was the most he'd said in the past two hours.

I nodded. "I'll see that they get watered too."

"And don't you go throwing out none of the corn pudding I cooked up the other day." He hacked a dry cough.

This time I shook my head.

Gent looked over at Ma like he had something more important on his mind. "Puttin' me here is a waste of the county's taxes," he muttered. "There ain't nothing more wrong than what I already got. It's them doctors looking to make more money."

Ma kissed him on the forehead. "See you bright and early tomorrow, Pop," she said, and she started for the door.

"No!" Gent's voice thundered across the sterile room. "You both got church to attend to first."

Ma turned around and smiled. "You going religious on me all of a sudden?" she asked.

"It's for your mother," he wheezed, drawing himself higher in the bed so he could better get his breath. "She'd want you to go."

Gent wasn't much of a churchgoer, but he always made certain Manny and I had a ride over and back, even if he had trouble finding his own way past the wooden cross that hung above the double doors.

"Gent's never coming back," I told Quentin later. It was just after dark when I went over to sit with him on the front stoop of his trailer. "I know he's not." And I started to cry.

"Etta May, your grandpa's coming home. Just like the doctor said."

I believed him. Maybe because I had to.

Quentin leaned against the trailer and began to sing.

> I've been ridin' on my pony.
> Till the night has turned to lonely.
> Now my heart beats to the songs of long ago . . .

The porch light was on, so I could see his eyes, deep blue-green like I figured the ocean would be when I finally got to see it someday.

Chapter Five

As we drove into the parking lot of the Calvary Church of God, I noticed that the church's double doors were flung wide open. Out front Brother Perry, the deacon, and Pastor Duncan were standing on either side of the entrance talking with the Harrisons.

Ma stepped out of the car, cigarette in hand, and took one final puff before throwing it away. She didn't seem to care if the pastor saw her smoking.

Together we headed for the front of the church.

"I remember the year Pop fixed up a big old Buick he'd bought and how proud I felt riding around in it," Ma said. "Especially on Sunday mornings, when he drove us up to the front of the church and I'd climb out behind Mama. Like I was a movie star getting out of my limo. I was younger than you then.

"I'd be wearing one of the ribboned dresses Mama made and my hair would be teased up like Little Orphan Annie's. Soon as I'd step out, though, I'd forget how movie stars are supposed to act and I'd bound up those same stairs." Ma giggled. "And Mama would call me back and remind me, 'Young ladies don't jump up the steps two at a time.'"

I tried to picture how she must have looked back then, and how she looked now, with her short skirt and loose-fitting blouse and dark hair that billowed around her shoulders. I noticed Brother Perry looking at us. Not at us really, at Ma.

I don't know what got into me then—maybe it was the way she was talking, or maybe it was the church, whitewashed and warmed by the sun, that made my brain get all mushy and forgetful of the hurt—but when she looped her arm around mine, I didn't pull away. We took the bottom steps two at a time, and I thought of Gent and Manny, younger and still strong, and Ma, girlish and pretty.

The sun drenched the land and sky with a brightness that made everything glow. All I wanted was to hug that glowy feeling to me forever.

Quentin, standing beside his pa, gaped at us as we entered. I wanted to run to him and throw my arms around him and tell him how happy I was feeling.

"Claire," began Pastor Duncan, taking Ma's hand and holding it between his bearlike paws. "Praise the Lord. It's been a long time. You and your family have been in our prayers. Brother Loomis doesn't come often enough but I know, from the many times he's driven your dear mother and Etta May to church, the Lord is in his heart. Working miracles, I say. Are you here for—"

"A visit." Ma smiled. "Good to see you, Pastor," she said as she walked away.

Gent had made it clear yesterday that, though he wanted us to attend church service, we were not to let on to anyone that he was in the hospital. Even if it was a few days and only for tests. Quentin knew, but he'd never tell a soul, not after I told him to keep quiet about it. Gent didn't like being the object of the Pastor's long-drawn-out prayers. Or so he'd say.

We sat in the last pew, right behind Quentin and Mr. Oaks. Quentin turned around to tell me something but he never got a chance because Pastor Duncan was already up at the altar telling us to turn to page eighty-nine in our music books. "Flowing like a river," we sang, and Quentin's voice pulled me into the current and carried me along. During the sermon I glanced at Ma, but from the quiet expression on her face, I couldn't tell what she was thinking. Was it about the times she'd sat right here, maybe in this very pew, with Manny?

Manny. A tingly feeling shot through me as I felt her presence blessing us from above. After the announcements and before the last song, Ma leaned over and took my arm. "I don't want to get tangled up here after service. Let's go," she whispered, getting up. There was nothing I could do but follow her through the double doors.

Just as Ma was pulling out of the parking lot, Quentin clambered down the church steps and motioned for us to wait up for him.

Ma stopped and I rolled my window the rest of the way down.

"Me and Pa are making hash browns and flapjacks after church. And . . . and we . . ." Quentin paused, his ears turning pink as he looked down at his feet. He was always shy around people he didn't know too well, and I could see that Ma being there was making him uncomfortable. "We was wondering if you'd eat with us."

Ma spoke up before I could say anything. "Thank you, Quentin. Etta May and I really do appreciate your invitation. But my father is expecting us right after church and I think this time we'll have to pass on it."

I could see that Quentin was disappointed. The glow I'd been feeling was fading.

"Hospital food won't be near as good as Mr. Oaks's cooking," I insisted as we drove away. "Besides, we could've called to let Gent know we'd be a little late."

"Pop is having this little procedure done and I thought we should be around to—"

"Procedure? What procedure?" I demanded.

"They have to drain his left lung. I'm sorry I didn't mention it yesterday, but I know how upset you get."

"You would be too if you weren't told!" I yelled.

Instead of raising her voice back, Ma controlled herself. "I only want to do what's best for Pop. The last thing he needs is for us to fall apart on him." She glanced over at me. "Please, baby . . . *please* try to understand."

I kept quiet because I decided it was better if Gent didn't see Ma and me all worked up. Not that I was one to fall apart. Besides, I didn't want to completely ruin what glowy feeling was left inside me.

At the hospital we found Gent with a thin tube running into his nose. It was connected to a clear plastic bag that hung off to the side of the bed. Even though he looked uncomfortable, I could tell from the way his eyes lit up how glad he was to see us.

Just then a nurse breezed into the room. "We need to drain this a little longer, Mr. Loomis," she said before checking the bag, which was slowly filling up with a yellowish liquid. "Are you breathing easier now?" When Gent nodded, she patted his arm and went out the door.

Gent wouldn't talk much because he said the tube, which ran down into his lung, was making his throat sore. "Worst sore throat in all my years," he sputtered in a hoarse voice.

We sat, Ma and me, on either side of him the rest of the day, reading magazines or talking quietly while Gent lay there in silence. Mostly our conversations were short, with Ma asking questions like, "Is Mr. Byrne still teaching English? He had a way of staring through you if you didn't come up with the answer he wanted."

"Yeah, he's still around."

When the nurses brought in the man who would be sharing Gent's room, we fell silent. I wasn't ready to let her think things between us were hunky-dory. Not yet, anyway.

Late that afternoon Doc Kelsy came to take the tube out, and I could tell Gent was awful glad to be rid of it. By the time Ma and I got ready to leave, Gent was sitting up in bed making an effort at conversation with his new roommate.

On the way home Ma drove up to the take-out

window at Tastee-Freez where we each ordered a hot fudge sundae with nuts sprinkled on top.

"Mmm, my favorite," I said, licking whipped cream off my spoon. "Gent is starting to act more like himself, don't you think, Ma?" I didn't intend to call her Ma to her face; it slipped out.

She smiled. "When he perked up enough to tell his roommate he didn't belong in the hospital, I figured he was feeling better too." She paused, then added, "I was thinking, Etta May, you and me haven't done anything like this—you know, fun things like eating ice cream sundaes alone together—in a long time. Not since—" Ma's voice broke and a sadness settled over her. "Not since before Mama passed away.

"I know I can't make up for lost time, but from now on I'm going to try harder. Oh, baby, you'll see." This time when she reached out to touch my cheek I didn't move away. "I'm making plans . . ."

A van full of kids spilled out into the parking lot, and though I wasn't certain, I thought I heard her add, "for us."

* * *

I should have known better than to think Ma and I would keep getting along. Monday after I got home from school it started to change. Ma had driven home from the hospital to take me back with her so we could be with Gent that night. I had just run up the front stoop and into the kitchen when the phone rang. "Hello . . . Claire?" said a man's voice on the other end of the line.

"Hold on, I'll get her for you." I put my hand over the receiver and called, "It's for you." When I didn't hear anything, I repeated louder, "The phone—it's for you."

When Ma came out of the bathroom, I wandered over to Gent's rocker by the window and peered out. But I didn't pay much attention to the Carrot Lady taking down sheets from the back clothesline or Zip digging around her bushes out front. Ma's conversation was a lot more interesting than anything going on outdoors.

". . . a week, maybe more. Eddie, did you remember to pay the rent?"

So she was shacking up with him. I don't know why, but it made me angry to think about her with this Eddie.

Ma turned her back to me then and started talking low into the phone. "Why are you doing this now? You've been drinking again, haven't you?" she said, raising her voice. "Don't deny it, Eddie, I know you have even from here. I can tell from . . . Look, I *need* at least a week with my family . . . *No! Please,* can't it wait till I get back next—"

I ran into my room and slammed the door shut.

Throwing myself on the bed, I tried to bite back the tears.

On the way over to the hospital, I asked, casual as you please so it wouldn't sound as though I was overly interested, "Who's Eddie?"

Ma didn't say anything at first, and I began to wonder if she had heard me.

"Who's Eddie?" I repeated.

She glanced over at me. "Just someone I know," she answered, her mouth flattening out in a straight line. I decided not to question her anymore about him.

We drove the next few miles in silence, Ma groping in her bag for a cigarette every ten minutes. "Pop's coming home tomorrow afternoon," she finally said. I got so excited over the good news I almost missed the rest of what she told me. "I was planning on staying longer," she added, "but something's come up at home, an emergency. And . . . and I have to get back. I'm sorry, baby."

"What emergency?" From Ma's conversation on the phone, I knew it had something to do with Eddie.

Ma didn't answer. Instead she said, "I don't know how long I'll be gone; I hope no more than a week or so."

From the way she was chain-smoking and fidgeting I decided that there was more. "What else did the doctors tell you?" I demanded.

Ma pulled into an empty space in the hospital parking ramp and turned off the engine. "There's nothing to tell, not till all the tests are back. Look, Pop is going on seventy and you know as well as I do he's not a healthy man." She crushed her cigarette in the car ashtray. "I have to go home for a while, and then I'll be back. I promise."

I wanted to ask, "What's going on?" But I held my tongue once more.

Chapter Six

Gent must be okay, I thought. Why else would the hospital let him go home? He slouched in the car seat beside Ma, only the tip of his cap showing above the headrest. When she pulled into the driveway, the rear right tire of the Volkswagen hit the curb and I felt a bump.

"The doctor says you're to take it easy, Pop," Ma reminded him when he insisted on carrying in one of the two bags of groceries we had picked up on the way home from the hospital. Even though I knew he'd taken the lighter one, he huffed up the stoop. I thought he was about to lose his balance, and I grabbed for him.

"Lord Almighty, girl," Gent said, shaking me loose. "I don't need somebody hanging on to me."

"It wasn't you, Gent. It's those chocolate chip cookies I was hanging on to so you don't dump them on the ground."

Inside, Gent leaned on the counter for support and took out the new inhaler he was to use when he couldn't get his breath. Then he shuffled over to his chair.

He didn't seem to mind Ma and me fussing over him. "You never had it so good," I teased after I got him a glass of water and switched the channel to his favorite game show. But I guess he wasn't in the mood to tease back, because he just sat staring, either at the TV set or out the window. Though I couldn't say he was looking at anything in particular. Even when Zip started digging near the trailer, he didn't pay any notice. So I shooed Zip away myself.

"Etta May, honey?" Ma began after the supper dishes had been cleared away and I was wiping the counter. She lit a cigarette and I noticed her hand shaking a tiny bit. Gent was on the couch, his thunderous snoring competing with a quiz show on TV. "Come outside so you and me can talk."

What did she want to talk about now? I wondered.

"Come on, Etta May. We'll clean it up later."

From the sound of her voice, I knew this time she must have something important on her mind. Putting the sponge back, I followed her out to the stoop where I sat beside her.

"It hasn't been easy, has it? With Mama gone it's just you and Pop living alone in this broken-down trailer. I never meant it to be this way." Ma's eyes looked puffy. "I already told you I have this emergency. But once I take care of things at home I'll be back. I promise, baby, for you and—"

"The trailer needs some work, but I can help Gent with that. Soon as he's up to it we'll fix the place just like before." Even though I didn't say anything about the leaky roof, I was worried over how we'd find the money to get it fixed. But I didn't want her to come back just because she felt sorry for us. She'll leave tomorrow just like she said, I thought, and that will be the last Gent and I will see of her for a long time, no matter what she says. That's the way it's always been with Ma.

"Why didn't I come sooner?" Ma said quietly, almost to herself. She ground her cigarette into the dirt.

"Possibly because of Eddie?" I wondered aloud.

Ma looked at me in a funny way. Soon as my words slipped out, I knew I'd gone and spoke too quickly again.

* * *

Early next morning, while Gent stood inside the screen door, I helped Ma pack up the Volkswagen. "You've got my work number too," she said, "so if you need me I want you to call. But if you need someone quick, you get hold of Mrs. Morales first."

If I needed help it wouldn't be the Carrot Lady I'd go to first off; it'd be Mr. Oaks.

"Etta May, are you listening?"

I nodded. She said a few more little things to me, waved at Gent, climbed into the car, and drove off.

The place got quiet, like after Manny died and it was just Gent and me to fill up the empty spaces. In a few minutes the school bus would come roaring down the road, but I didn't know if I should leave Gent alone. "I could stay home and—"

"No," he said, waving me on. Then Gent turned on the TV and sat in his chair, staring at the screen. Before Manny died it wasn't like Gent to sit around all day. He'd be up at the first sign of light so he could tend his roses in the cooler part of the day.

"You want me to water the roses when I get back?" I'd taken care of them while he was in the hospital. Even though he was home now, springtime could be hard on him, as far as his wheezing went, and I knew he'd never ask for help.

"Too little water is worse than no water," he'd once told me. "You got to wet the roots down good, Etta May." And if I happened to sprinkle a leaf, he'd bark out, "Keep them leaves dry!" The whole time he would stand over me like a mother hen clucking out orders. After a while, though, he trusted me to do it by myself.

When Gent didn't say anything, I added, "If you want, I could nail up some of the stakes that have fallen over and maybe do some weeding too." I was hoping he'd tell me to stop bothering and go on to school so he could do it himself. Instead, he looked up at me silently for a moment before turning back to the TV.

"*Etta May!*" called Quentin from outside.

"I gotta go now." I went up to Gent and, when he held his grizzly cheek out for me just like he always did, I kissed him twice. "There's a sandwich in the fridge, and don't forget to take your medicine at noon," I said before going out the door.

After school I found Gent the way I had left him that morning, still in his pajama bottoms and his hair sticking up every which way around his bald spot. The medicine bottles had been moved, so I figured he had taken his pills, but the sandwich was untouched. "Well, looky here," I said, pulling the wax paper–wrapped sandwich out of the fridge and holding it up so Gent could see it. "Perfectly good baloney sandwich that's just taking up space. Guess I'll have to throw it away." I started for the garbage bin under the sink. "Yup, sure is a shame throwing away good food like—"

"Nobody said anything about not eating it!" called Gent from his chair. "Now you put that back in the refrigerator where it belongs."

Grinning, I put it back beside a carton of eggs. After checking the other shelves to see what I could make for supper later, I noticed a slice of ham left over from the other day. "How about an onion and ham omelet for supper?" I called. Gent grunted his approval. Then I grabbed two oatmeal cookies and went to the back of the trailer to change into my old jeans and sweatshirt. While I was back there, someone knocked on the door. Gent took forever to answer, but as soon as I heard the Carrot Lady's voice, I threw on my sweatshirt and hurried out.

Mrs. Morales stood beside the door with a pie tin in her hands. "I was just telling your grandfather," she began, looking around as if she expected to be invited to stay. "Now that he's home from the hospital, he might want some good home cooking."

I took the pie tin from her and put it on the counter. Then I swung around and put my hand on the knob so she'd get the idea to leave. "Thanks, Mrs. Morales."

"That was neighborly of you," said Gent, lifting the plastic wrap off the pie and sniffing it. "Hmmm, cherry." He grinned.

"Last season was the best we had in years, just the right amount of moisture and sunshine. Picked them at Hanson's Orchard and froze them myself."

Gent nodded. "I could tell there was something extra special about *these* cherries." He winked at her. "Well, now I'm the one not being neighborly. Why don't you come right in and sit a spell?"

Mrs. Morales breezed past me and plunked herself on the couch. I yanked the door open and tramped outside. On the way to the road I kicked one of Gent's rose plants. "'Why don't you come right in and sit a spell?'" Lord, sometimes the man could be so infuriating. Mr. Fisher used *infuriate* once as his Word of the Day. It means "to make furious or enrage." Well, Gent was good on both counts. He wouldn't even touch my baloney sandwich or show one bit of gratitude for what I was trying to do. But he sure could be sweet and talkative to people like the Carrot Lady.

I heard the squeal of bike tires braking. "I'm going over to the mall," said Quentin. "You want me to pick you up anything?" When I shook my head, he took off again. I watched as he flew down to the main road and around the corner. He was going all the way over to the mall and back just so he could drool over a dumb electric guitar he didn't have a prayer of getting. How unfair it all was.

I waited till I was certain Mrs. Morales had gone home before I went back inside to start supper. The whole time I cooked up the omelet I didn't say a word, until I called Gent in to eat. During supper he mostly just picked at his food. "You saving up for that extra special cherry pie?" I sounded out the last four words real slow like Gent did when he said them to Mrs. Morales.

"Now, Etta May, you don't have to raise your temper none. That pie is for both of us."

"It's not the stupid pie I care about," I snapped back. "It's you. You've been sitting around here gloomy like the Grinch Who Stole Christmas. Just sitting and watching those dumb game shows. And then Mrs. Morales shows up and you're all smiles." I got up, left my dishes in the sink, and went off to my room at the back of the trailer.

After a few minutes there was a knock on my door. "You all right, Etta May?" I could hear the hurt in Gent's voice.

"I'm okay . . . just doing some homework," I lied. Why did I say things I didn't mean? It was Gent who usually got the brunt of it. Hardly ever Ma. We were more like strangers, Ma and me. That's the way it was. And then I wondered, was that the way it would always be?

After I heard Gent walk away, I wiped my eyes on my sleeve and went into the kitchen. The pie was still untouched, so I cut two pieces and brought him one.

"You get to water them roses like you said?" asked Gent, taking a bite. "Can't expect them to bloom their best if they don't get proper care."

Chapter Seven

"What's that you're listening to?" I asked Quentin. We had just stepped off the school bus and Quentin, who had on a pair of earphones, was humming a tune I'd never heard.

"Garth Brooks's newest song," he answered, unplugging the earphones and turning up the volume to his transistor so I could hear.

I listened awhile. "You're as good as Garth Brooks any ol' day." Quentin liked to hear me say that. His ears turned pink and he acted like it was no big deal. "Shoot, Quentin, you can sing better than a lot of those big stars from Nashville."

When Quentin sang, the air itself seemed to quiver. It was because of his ma. Even without him ever telling me, I knew he sang for her.

"WHUG," said the announcer. "Huggin' country, coming to you straight from Liberty's finest country music station. One-oh-nine-point-five on your dial."

We turned onto our road and I saw something out front of my place that made me look twice to be sure I wasn't dreaming it up. Gent was on his knees digging around a rosebush.

"Swing your partner on down to Liberty High School auditorium on Saturday, May thirtieth, for Liberty's first annual Jumpin' Jamboree Talent Show," continued the announcer.

"Hey, listen," I said to Quentin.

"Buy your tickets now so you don't miss out on huggin' country fun," said the announcer. "And if it's talent you got, folks, call us at 555-4807 to set up an audition for the show. Two hundred-dollar prizes awarded for the best local talent. And to top it off, the show will be carried live on our own cable station, Channel 12, WKBW, right here in Liberty."

I forgot about Gent's newfound energy for a minute and dug in my book bag for a pencil and paper. "Five-five-five-four-eight-oh-seven," I repeated over and over till I wrote it down. Then, grinning, I waved the number at Quentin. "That Hank Williams electric guitar you've been wanting so bad? Well, I'd say getting it is beginning to look awful good."

"Not if I got to do what I think you want me to."

"I know what you're thinking," I went on. "You don't have any backup guitars or such. But you got your voice, don't you? Then you don't need anything else. Hey, how about singing that new song of yours? You know, the one about the cowboy riding in the night." I stopped because of the way Quentin was staring at me—like a deer frozen in the middle of the road looking at a car's headlights. "Come on, Quentin, it won't be that bad. When you're up on that stage, just pretend you're looking out at a bunch of Etta May faces and you'll be okay." Crossing my eyes, I stuck out my tongue at him. "Then the hardest thing you'll have to do is keep from laughing." We stopped and I waited for him to answer.

Thrusting his hands deep into his pockets, Quentin began making tiny circles in the dirt road with his boot. Finally he shook his head. "It's not gonna work, Etta May. I . . . I just know it ain't." And he started shuffling down the road to his place.

"It will too if only you'll use your imagination," I called after him. But when he kept shaking his head, I added, "Shoot, Quentin, don't you want that guitar bad enough?" Even though he didn't answer I wasn't about to drop the subject.

"That boy's got a mind of his own," said Gent, looking up at me from where he crouched beside his favorite rosebush. "Don't you go meddling in his affairs."

But he does too need somebody to look after him, I almost blurted out, *just like you, Gent.* Instead, I said, "I'm only trying to . . . to encourage him. That's all."

"Be sure it's no more'n that," grunted Gent as he cut off the end of a rose shoot with his pruning knife. "You might say I encourage these plants to be strong so they don't lose their beauty. If I tried to make them into something they ain't, girl, I'd do them more harm than good."

I wasn't listening. I was remembering another time long ago. Manny wouldn't let me play outside alone then, so whenever Gent got ready to work on his roses, I would ask to go too. The nod always came and I would scamper out the door. Soon I'd grow tired of what I was playing, though, and settle down beside Gent. He'd keep right on working as though he hadn't noticed. His hands, soil-stained and rough, would reach out to each rose with a touch so gentle that love itself sprang from his fingertips. Those very same hands that took care of Manny and me.

I never could sit still long without asking questions. "What's that one called?" I would say, pointing.

"Grace Abounding." And before I could ask about another, he would go through all their names for me. There were Golden Jewel and King Arthur and Queen Elizabeth and Red Dandy and so many more I would forget which was which and later I would ask again. But there was one I never had to ask about. This rose I knew was special. Gent always said its name the way Pastor Duncan said Jesus' name, stretching out the beginning sound. "Summer Song." Then with a smile, he'd repeat, "Summer Song. Like your grandma's hair."

It seemed strange that Manny once had hair the color of summer. Gent called it coppery yellow, and I had wished that I too could have been born with hair that color. But mine was dark, like Ma's.

The ground was still damp and spongy from the spring rains so I went inside to get a plastic bag. I spread the bag out and sat down near Gent, hugging my knees to me. As I watched his hands move quickly among the roses, cutting here and there, I felt like that little girl again asking the same questions. "How do you know where to cut?"

He looked at me as though he was wondering why I asked. "Once you know how, it ain't hard," he finally answered, holding the tip of a shoot in his left hand. He was wheezing, not too hard but hard enough to sound like the hiss of a teakettle working up steam. "You got to cut it right here, above an outward-growing bud like this one. And snipping any which way won't do any good. The cut's got to be smooth with an angle so the rain runs down away from the bud. And not too close or it won't heal proper."

Summer Song was already pruned, its dead leaves and branches taken off and the ends of its shoots cut smooth with the care only Gent could give. The wind came up and I wrapped my jacket tighter around me. Gent was sitting on the ground now, his shoulders moving up and down as he sucked in each breath.

"The wind is making it too cold to work," I said. "I'll pick up out here while you start supper." I started gathering the loose stems and deadwood around the roses, keeping my eyes off Gent. Even though I wanted to put my arms around him and help him up the three steps, I knew he'd never let me. While I finished cleaning up and putting his pruning knife away in the shed out back, he slowly made his way into the trailer.

*   *   *

"Auditions are next Thursday night," I told Quentin the next day over lunch. I slipped it in while I was telling him about Ma's phone call last night, so maybe he wouldn't pick up on it right away. The idea was for it to seep slowly into his thoughts. Sort of like a subliminal message. Mrs. Higbee told us all about those in health class last week. The idea is simple. Pictures or sounds are hidden in things like a video or movie. Then the image is flashed by so fast—in a split second—that you don't even know it's there. But this is the interesting part: that image gets planted in your subconscious mind.

"Ma never did say exactly *when* she'd be back," I added. "All she said is, *soon.* Do you suppose she means it this time?"

For somebody who's supposed to be slow, Quentin caught on pretty quick. His face got red all over. "Etta May? You're not making any plans for me to audition."

"It crossed my mind. Oh, look at you, Quentin, acting like a big baby over nothing." I leaned both elbows on the lunch table and looked him in the face. "What harm would it do if you went to watch? You know, see how it's done." I figured once we got there he'd change his mind.

Quentin blinked twice before drawling out, "No harm, I guess. But I can't go anyhow because Pa works nights."

"I already figured on that. I asked Gent to take us." I poked him in the arm and grinned.

Gent hadn't exactly said he would, but he hadn't said he wouldn't, either. Last night I told him Quentin needed a ride to the auditions. He said, "You talking that boy into something he don't want to do?"

It wasn't that Quentin didn't want to audition; it was that he was too scared even to try. You might say I was encouraging him to do what he truly wanted. So I shook my head. "We can do our grocery shopping Thursday night instead of Wednesday. That way we don't have to make two trips into town."

"Etta May?" One of Gent's wiry brows arched higher. "Don't you go planning on something I ain't agreed to."

Chapter Eight

"He's been working on his roses," I told Ma when she called the following Sunday night and asked about Gent. I was excited about giving her the good news. "He's out there 'most every day now just like he used to before Manny . . ." I couldn't say the word out loud because, in a way. Manny would always be here with Gent and me. So I went on: "That's got to mean he's feeling a whole lot better."

Except for some music in the background, it got awful quiet on the other end. Finally Ma said, "You just make sure he doesn't overdo it. You hear me, Etta May?"

"I hear you." In the background came the sound of a man's voice. Eddie, I thought, Eddie's there with her. "You alone?"

"The stereo's on."

But it sounded like more than just the stereo to me.

"Look, Etta May, I can't come back any sooner than next Saturday. But if something should come up before then and you need to get hold of somebody quick, you—"

"I *know.*"

Ma's conversations over the phone were never much more than a few minutes because of the long-distance charge. But this time she seemed to want to talk even less than usual. "So, you doing okay, honey?" she finally asked. When I told her I was, she said her goodbyes and hung up.

Ma had finally set a day when she'd be back, and I should have been glad. Instead, I felt uneasy. I guess I had thought she'd understand how important it was that Gent had started taking an interest in his roses again. Only she hadn't understood at all.

During the week, Gent didn't say any more about Thursday. I decided it was best not to make a big issue over it, especially since he hadn't told me straight out that he wouldn't drive Quentin and me over to the auditions. Besides, it would probably only make him "dig in his heels," as Manny would say whenever he'd set his mind on something. Every day, though, I made certain the roses got watered and the place picked up.

Wednesday after supper, Gent carried his plate to the sink where I was scraping the dishes before putting them in the pan to soak. He had barely touched his food. I was about to remind him of all the times he'd tell me to eat till my plate was "clean as a whisker." But I never did get a chance.

"Get your jacket, Etta May," Gent ordered, cool and casual as you please. He took the weekly grocery list off the fridge and picked up the truck keys.

I whirled to face him. "What do you mean, get my jacket? We're going shopping *tomorrow* like we planned."

Gent shook his head. "I already told you, girl, that boy don't need any meddling in his affairs."

I wanted to throw the dishpan of hot, soapy water at him. Instead, I threw his plate into the sink, where it shattered against the edge.

Gent stood there a moment looking dumbfounded, then got his jacket and went out the door. I poked the kitchen curtains aside and watched him slowly climb into the pickup. He sat for a long time, his head bowed and his shoulders slumped over. I figured he was waiting for me to come out. For all I cared, he could stay inside that rickety ol' truck till the floor rotted out.

Going to my room, I turned the radio way up and sat on my bed. How could Gent say I was interfering, when I was only trying to help? Quentin needed a nudge in the right direction, that's all. Why couldn't Gent understand that?

With the radio booming, I knew I wouldn't hear the kitchen door open when Gent finally came back inside. So I got up to see if he was in his chair yet, and when he wasn't, I glanced out the kitchen window. The pickup was gone. I stood there, staring at that empty spot and thinking of Gent on his way to Liberty. A hot bolt suddenly pierced my heart and I started to cry.

Ever since Manny got too sick to do the grocery shopping, Gent and I had gone together. It was an arrangement we had fallen into, like taking turns fixing supper.

I wiped my eyes with the back of my hand and wandered over to Gent's chair by the front window. A light from Mrs. Morales's place glowed in the twilight. After I sat looking out at the road a long time it finally occurred to me what to do. I picked up the pie tin that had been on the kitchen counter since the other day and went outside.

Next door, I bolted up the steps, pausing on the stoop before pushing the buzzer. A nearby curtain pushed aside and the Carrot Lady peered out at me. A look of surprise crossed her face. Seeing me there must have been quite a shock, since I'd always done my best to avoid her place. Grinning, I waved the pie tin to let her know the reason for my unexpected visit. She opened the door wearing a yellow chenille bathrobe that was worn in a few choice spots. I teetered on the threshold a moment, wondering if I was doing the right thing. I knew how Gent felt, and I also knew how sore he'd be if he ever found out what I was about to do.

"Isn't this a nice surprise?" She clasped her stubby hands together and beamed at me before taking the pie tin in one hand and grabbing me with the other. The place looked heavy, with rose-colored velvet drapes and a thick carpet. The furniture was boxy with spindly legs that didn't look able to support much weight—like the Carrot Lady herself.

"Come right in, Etta May, and make yourself at home," she said, leading me over to a flowered overstuffed chair. "I'll make us some hot chocolate."

"Yes, thank you," I answered, as I sat in the chair, sinking deep between the high armrests. I felt imprisoned in its embrace. A crazy notion popped into my head of the Carrot Lady luring unsuspecting people over with her pies and then holding them captive in her furniture.

The whole time Mrs. Morales was in the kitchen she kept talking about "my Carl," as though Mr. Morales were still alive. In fact, he had died four years ago, not long after they moved into Sunshine Pines. "I hope I didn't get this too hot," she said, handing me a steaming mug. "My Carl always said, 'Now, Anna, you don't have to scald a person's mouth just to prove it's called *hot* chocolate. You might better call it *warm* chocolate from now on.'" When she giggled, the loose skin under her neck moved like waves fanning out from shore.

I took a sip and wondered how I was going to work the conversation away from her Carl and toward the true reason I'd come. Across from me on a round table was a picture of the Crucifixion, with a gold cross in front of it. On either side were framed photographs. In the black and white picture on the left were two identical-looking boys in swimsuits standing on a beach. On the right was a larger, color picture of a man and woman with three little kids. The man had dark curly hair and close-set eyes like the twin boys. Mrs. Morales must have noticed me looking, because she went over to the table and sat in a nearby chair. "My Johnny and his family," she said, picking up the picture and rubbing her fingers over the glass. "They live in Portland, Oregon, now. Five years it's been since they packed up and left. I've only held my granddaughter once." She sighed and her whole body seemed to rise up out of the chair.

"The summer after he finished school, Johnny and a friend drove across the country and after that all he could talk about was Oregon. 'You got to see it, Ma,' he'd tell me. 'Snow-topped mountains and forests so beautiful it catches your breath.'" Mrs. Morales paused, her chin trembling a tiny bit. "He wants me to live with them, but I don't want to be a burden."

A burden, I thought, and wondered if Ma considered Gent a burden. I figured I probably was, but it had never occurred to me that Gent could be too.

Mrs. Morales put the picture back. "I see your grandfather working outdoors again. Even the Andersons mentioned to me the other day how they noticed he's not been out much. Till now, of course. I told them, 'Dan couldn't stay away from his roses anymore.' I've never seen anybody give such care like your grandpa. The way he can make those roses of his end up looking like they came straight out of *Home and Garden*." Mrs. Morales put her empty mug on the table. "Now that he's up and about more, your grandfather must be feeling better."

I nodded stupidly at her, almost forgetting the reason I was there. "Well, actually he's not to overdo things . . . orders from the doctor. You know, things like working on his roses or a lot of driving." I wasn't exactly lying; after all, Gent *was* supposed to take it easy.

"Oh, yes, yes, I do understand. My Carl would *never* listen either."

"It was so nice of you to bring that pie over and look in on Gent when he was sick, Quentin and I wanted to invite you to the talent show. You've never heard Quentin sing, but I can tell you, Mrs. Morales, he's got a voice that will break your heart in two. Smooth like silk. Anyway, WHUG is putting on a Jumpin' Jamboree Talent Show over at Liberty High. Quentin's good enough to sing in it. I just know he is.

"But if he can't get to the auditions tomorrow night he won't make it on the show. And it's really important he does. Then maybe Quentin's ma will hear him on the TV and miss him and his daddy so that she'll come back." I stopped to catch my breath before going on. "Like I said, Gent has to take it easy now, so he can't be driving Quentin and me all the way over to the auditions in Liberty. And with his pa working nights," I added, shaking my head, "Quentin won't ever get the chance again."

"Well, now, don't you and Quentin let it worry you one second more. That Ford of mine hasn't been getting much of a workout lately anyway. Mostly filling up the driveway with nowhere to go." Mrs. Morales smiled and I noticed how brightly her eyes sparkled.

Chapter Nine

Though I couldn't be sure, I figured Gent took his time getting back from Liberty just so I'd be crazy with worry. As soon as headlights flashed past our drive, I jumped back from the kitchen window and shot down the hall into the bathroom. When I heard him in the kitchen, I moseyed on out.

Gent was on a stool holding onto the counter with both hands. Beside him was a bag of groceries. From the few things inside, I knew he had told the checkout girl to pack the bags light. I started for the closet to get my jacket. "I'll carry in the rest—"

"Never you mind, girl. I got 'em in the first place, so I might as well bring 'em in myself."

Instead of doing what I knew was right, I turned and stomped to my room, slamming the door. But after he went to bed I heard him wheezing from the other side of the wall. In and out. In and out. And I lay there in the chill of the night struggling to breathe for him.

The next morning as I was finishing my breakfast, Gent came into the kitchen and made us each a steaming mug of coffee. Then he sat across the counter from me, his unshaven face pale as new plaster, and bit into the toasted muffin I had left out for him.

I spooned a teaspoon of sugar into my coffee and stirred. Neither of us had spoken since last night, and I knew the longer it went on the harder it would be to start up a conversation again. "I didn't mean to throw the plate so hard it'd break," I said, speaking into the mug. But it wasn't the broken plate. Even though I wasn't sure how to say it, I wanted him to know it was his going off without me that mattered.

Gent, grunting out something I didn't catch, took another bite. It must have gone down wrong because the next thing I knew he was having a bad spell.

I grabbed for him.

Shaking me off, Gent got up and stumbled for the bathroom. "My inhaler," he gasped, and I ran to get it.

Then I went to the kitchen and started fingering through the Ks in the phone book. "Kelsy . . .

Kelsy," I muttered under my breath. Just as I was about to dial Doc Kelsy's number Gent walked into the kitchen.

"You making a social call?" Gent panted out each word between breaths. He was trying to show me he was okay and he didn't need help from anybody, especially Doc. With his dentures removed, his cheeks and lips shrunk back into pale shadows. He grinned at me, a silly, toothless grin just like he used to do when I was little. Only back then he took his teeth out on purpose just to make me giggle. Manny always got after him: "That's no way to act in front of a little girl!" And he'd answer, "Now, Manny, I'm just funnin' with Etta May."

"Doc's got to know about—"

Gent popped his teeth back into his mouth. "I'm all right, Etta May." He grinned again.

Even though I wasn't so sure, I put the phone book back and went to rinse my dishes in the sink. But I kept an eye on him till Quentin came by and hollered for me.

Gent shook his head. "When will that boy ever learn to knock?"

I grabbed my books, gave Gent a peck on his cheek, and started for the door. "I want you to promise you'll take it easy today, Gent. I won't leave till you do."

"Take it easy? You sound like your ma. This ol' body will tell me what I can and can't do."

"Etta May!" Quentin hollered again. "We're gonna be late!"

I didn't budge.

"Got things to tend to," Gent mumbled. When I still didn't move, he waved me on with his hand. "I'm telling you, girl, there's nothin' to worry over." He turned to face me, and I noticed that the crevices lining his forehead seemed deeper. "You go on to school now so I can have some peace and quiet around here."

Even though I didn't want to go, I felt my legs carry me out the door and down the steps. Quentin was already halfway to the bus stop.

By the time I got on the bus Mrs. Traub was waiting with her pencil-thin eyebrows scrunched up. "I got a schedule to keep," she barked, swinging the door shut behind me.

Ignoring her, I went over to the seat beside Quentin and slid in.

"Plans for tonight have changed some."

Quentin turned toward me with a blank look on his face.

"The audition," I snapped. "Don't you remember? It's tonight."

"I know that, Etta May." Quentin stretched the words out like he always did, as though measuring each sound, but he spoke with a force I wasn't used to. He blinked twice before going on. "If your grandpa can't take me, it's okay, 'cause I don't think I want to—"

"You didn't say you wouldn't go. You're not breaking your word, are you?" After all I'd done, I wasn't going to let him back out now.

"'Change of plans,' that's what you just said, Etta May. 'Change of plans.' I heard so myself."

"I said plans have changed *some*. Gent can't take us, that's all. You know how he's supposed to rest up more than he's been doing. Anyhow that's not going to matter because you'll never guess what happened." I grinned at him. "The Carrot La—I mean, Mrs. Morales said she'd be real glad to take us." I decided not to say "The Carrot Lady." With her doing Quentin and me a favor, it didn't seem respectful.

Quentin gave me a puzzled look. "Aren't you always telling me to pay her no mind?"

"Shoot, Quentin. I just meant you shouldn't go and tell her certain things you don't want to get around. That's all. But you got to be neighborly, don't you? Especially since she's the one who suggested taking us in the first place. I couldn't possibly say no when she was neighborly enough to go out of her way."

"But . . . but how did she know?"

I shrugged. "Guess Mrs. Morales happened to

hear about us needing a ride." Before he had a chance to ask any more questions I didn't want to answer, I got in one of my own. "I been wondering. You know how your ma always listened to nothing but country music? Well, you suppose she might tune in to the Jamboree when it's on? Channel 12 is televising it, remember? If your ma's anywhere near enough to get it, I know she'll be watching." Pausing, I looked over at Quentin gazing out the bus window.

"I've been wondering," I continued. "It's just wondering, you understand, 'cause I know what you said about not trying out and all. Anyway, I've been wondering what your mama would do if she saw you on that show. Kinda gives me the goose bumps just thinking about it."

Quentin had told me how his ma used to sing to him when he was little. Maybe that was why he liked making up his own songs and singing himself. From the way he looked, I figured he was thinking of her right now, about the way she was before she left. He once told me how her songs made him feel. "Like floating on Trainor's Pond," he'd said. "Nothing is more gentle than those water arms . . . or my mama's singin'."

I had asked him then how he came up with words that were as good as any poem I'd read in school. It was the same with his songs.

But he had just shrugged it off.

The whole time I was talking, Quentin kept looking out that window. He didn't once say anything, till we got to school. As soon as the bus pulled up to the curb he turned to me. "I don't recall you telling me when we got to leave for the audition tonight," he said.

His words made me feel glowy inside, like Gent probably felt every time he planted a new rosebush. Once when I was five or six I watched him put in a whole row of tiny plants. "Beautiful, ain't it, Etta May?" he had said, packing down the soil with his brown, callused hands. His face shone bright as the sun overhead.

At the time I didn't see how a stick with a bunch of prickers all over could ever be beautiful. Only later, after those sticks grew and grew and the first buds began to unfold, did I understand what he'd been talking about.

In a way, I had just planted one of them brand-new rosebushes.

Chapter Ten

How would I leave tonight without Gent finding out what I was up to? I couldn't possibly say I was going to Mrs. Morales's place. Before I could escape out the door, Gent would be all over me demanding: "What are you goin' over there for?" He knew how I felt about Mrs. Morales.

What *was* my reason? The chance of me speaking the bare truth was as good as Mr. Spinelli, the owner of Sunshine Pines, telling everybody their rent was going down.

But I wasn't about to tell an outright lie, either; not with Pastor Duncan's sermons on hell and fire rumbling around in my head. If only I could come up with something that didn't wander too far from the God Almighty truth. Finally, after thinking on it all day, I got an idea.

I asked Mrs. Morales to pick us up at Quentin's. Gent didn't question me when I told him I was going over there.

"You wouldn't believe all the homework," I said, loading my arms with the pile of books I'd taken home. "Quentin wanted help real bad, so I'd better get on over there." Since I didn't exactly say what kind of help I was about to give, it seemed all right by the pastor's standards. "Looks like I won't be back for some time."

"Etta May?"

I held my breath.

"Close that door tight, you hear? I don't want the wind taking hold and banging it into the side again."

I glanced over at Gent. He sat in his chair, leaning forward, with his elbows on the armrests. The faded blue sweater he wore hung from his shoulders and arms. I felt sad about fibbing to him, but I couldn't stop myself from going out the door.

Quentin was waiting for me. I noticed right off that his unruly hair was slicked back, and the black rawhide boots he always wore now had enough spit and shine to brighten up the whole place.

I dropped the books on the kitchen counter. Quentin's trailer was a lot like ours, with a rounded counter in the kitchen area and a postage stamp–sized living room at the front.

"What are you doing with all them books?" he asked.

I was trying to come up with a good reason for carrying so many books around when I glanced out the side window and saw Mrs. Morales's Ford heading down the road. "Come on," I said, grabbing Quentin's arm, "our ride's here." By the time Mrs. Morales pulled up front, we were standing by the edge of the driveway. Even though her car was a bit newer than Gent's pickup, I had to admit it wasn't in much better condition.

We slid into the front seat. I ended up crushed between Mrs. Morales on one side and Quentin on the other, though I couldn't blame skinny ol' Quentin for taking up most of the space.

Soon as the car pulled away, I dropped my opened shoulder bag on the floor, so I'd have an excuse to get down out of sight when we passed our trailer. "Quentin, can you help me look for—" I started, grabbing him by his jacket collar and hauling him down with me. On the way down, he banged his head on the glove compartment.

"Ouch!"

Mrs. Morales put on the brakes and Quentin thumped his head again. "Oh, dear me," Mrs. Morales said. "Perhaps I should stop at home and fix up a cold compress."

Popping my head up just enough so I could see out the window, I noticed we had stopped in full view of Gent, who was probably straining right now to see what was going on. "He's okay," I said and stuffed myself back into my doubled-up position. "Aren't you?" I poked Quentin in the arm.

"Ah-umm."

"Look, there's my quarter! Can you reach it for me, Quentin?" After we pulled away, I said, "I think we got everything now."

Mrs. Morales wasn't one to put much weight on the gas pedal. Soon we were at the head of a line of cars that stretched back so far I felt like we were the hearse in a funeral possession.

By the time we got to Liberty, the school parking lot was almost full. I wondered if seeing all those cars would get Quentin's nerves so jangled up that he'd change his mind.

That's when I started talking nonstop about any dumb thing just to keep him from getting stage fright. "You should see the posters Mr. Fisher put up on the back wall of our homeroom," I told Mrs. Morales. "He's always doing that, putting up new posters and taking down old ones. Anyway, one of them is a picture of this lake with a mountain behind it." I held the side door to the school open. "It's a real pretty scene, isn't it, Quentin?"

He shrugged. "Yeah, real pretty."

I turned to Mrs. Morales. "It made me think of the mountains you were telling me about where your son lives." Then to Quentin, I explained,

"Mrs. Morales's son lives in Oregon. I'll bet his house is near a mountain like that one too."

Mrs. Morales giggled. "From what Johnny tells me, they have a lot of mountains. But he lives in Portland, so I suppose he has to drive a ways to get to one."

"I've never seen mountains like that." I sighed. "But then I've never been anywhere much beyond Liberty. How about you, Quentin?" We were inside the auditorium now and I could see he was not one bit interested in what I was saying. I nudged him. "Quentin?" But I spoke low this time because I was afraid any loud noise might make him jump.

At the front of the auditorium a line of people waited to pick up their numbers. It made me think of Delino's Bakery, where you had to get a ticket from the counter and then wait for your number to be called. After Manny got sick, Gent and I went to Delino's once and stood around for ten minutes before we realized what was going on.

"Looks like everybody is down front," I said. Quentin acted unsure. I grabbed his arm and we started down a long aisle.

Quentin ended up with number twenty-eight. By the time the auditions began, he was as tense as an animal about to be captured. "Aren't you glad you're not first?" I whispered. "By the time you get in front of the judges they'll be warmed up."

I couldn't believe all the people who thought they could sing. Some of them were so awful they made my eardrums ring. Everybody was told to sing a few stanzas, and if they were any good the judges would let them go on a little longer. None of it seemed to bother Mrs. Morales because she clapped at the end of each person's turn like it was Kenny Rogers performing.

When number twenty-seven was called Quentin started shaking so much I thought he was going to rattle his seat loose from the floor. I put my hand on his. "All you got to remember is to look at me. Just me. You do that and you'll be okay." I kept whispering to him, telling him it was no different than when we were at home and I was there to listen. When his number was called he somehow got up on the stage. He stood in front of the microphone with his hands stuffed in his pockets, staring at the floor.

"Son, you got any taped backup music?" asked a man with curly red hair.

After shuffling back and forth a bit, Quentin shook his head.

"All right then," the red-haired man added, nodding at Quentin to begin before peering down at the papers he was holding. But Quentin didn't move; he stood frozen in his cocoon of silence while people talked and moved around backstage.

"Lord Almighty," I mumbled.

The man glanced back at Quentin, waving him on.

Still Quentin didn't move.

"We don't have all day, son. We'll have to go on to the next—"

Before he could say another word, I was on my feet singing in a quivery voice, "I've been riding on my pony—"

And then I heard Quentin, his voice clear and strong as a meadowlark.

> *Till the night has turned to lonely.*
> *Now my heart beats to the songs of long ago.*
> *My mama sang them to me.*
> *And I still remember clearly,*
> *The times my mama sang so long ago . . .*

He stared at me, singing and staring hard as though it wasn't me there at all, but his mama. Then the silence swallowed up his last note, and my eyes ached from holding back the tears.

Chapter Eleven

"Stop acting so gloomy," I told Quentin on the way back from the audition. "I just know they'll call you." Only the people who were phoned within the next couple of days would get to sing at the Jamboree.

But Quentin, sitting beside me, kept shaking his head. "Everybody else had backup music."

"A lot of them used canned music or just a guitar. Besides, did the judges let everybody sing all the way through their song, the way they let you? No siree. You'll get that electric guitar, someday. But for now, you use what you got. Even if it's nothing but your own voice."

"Etta May's right," said Mrs. Morales.

Then it occurred to me that Quentin had changed his mind one hundred eighty degrees, and I started to laugh.

"What's so funny?" asked Quentin.

"You worrying over whether or not you're going to get to sing at the Jamboree, when just the other day you acted like nothing could drag you to the auditions."

Quentin shrugged. "I only did like you said, Etta May. I looked at you the whole time."

"My Johnny and his friends started up a band," said Mrs. Morales. "It was so long ago I'd almost forgotten. Back when he was in tenth grade, I think." The car slowed to a crawl.

I glanced at the clock on the dashboard. It was going on nine-thirty, late by Gent's standards. I hoped he hadn't called up Quentin's place. If only Mrs. Morales would stop talking about her son and step on it so we could get back before ten. Instead, she pulled up to Dino's Diner along Route 5.

"I could use a cup of coffee."

"But we have to get back before—"

"Etta May, if you think your grandfather's going to worry, we can give him a call. Same goes for you, Quentin. I'm treating the both of you to ice cream, and I won't take no for an answer."

"Pa's not home yet, 'cause he's working the second shift," Quentin answered.

I shrugged as though it wouldn't matter either way. Then I kept quiet.

We sat at a booth in the back of the diner.

Quentin and I both ordered milkshakes, but he wanted strawberry and I wanted chocolate. Mrs. Morales ordered only coffee because she said any kind of dessert was her downfall. "Let's see now, what were we talking about?" she asked after the waitress brought her coffee. "Oh, yes, Johnny's band. Every day after school the boys practiced at our house. Always so much going on then; the house was never quiet, not with Johnny and his friends around. What noise they could make! Sometimes Carl and me had to leave just to keep our sanity." She giggled. "But my Johnny didn't have the talent. Not like you do, Quentin."

The waitress brought our milkshakes.

I wanted to get back to the car as quick as possible, so I dove into the ice cream.

"Etta May is right." Mrs. Morales smiled. "You have a voice like silk."

I could tell Quentin was uncomfortable with all the attention, because his ears were turning pink.

Then, looking over at me, Mrs. Morales added, "Thank goodness you told me how much Quentin needed a ride. Or I never would have—"

"I have to use the bathroom," I blurted out. Jumping up from my seat, I scrambled for a door on the back wall with a woman's face painted on it. I paced back and forth between the two stalls, thinking of what I'd tell Quentin.

But when I got back he never asked, or even looked at me. All the way home Quentin didn't say another word, not even when Mrs. Morales left me off in front of my trailer. I hung around outside till she came back from dropping off Quentin.

"I . . . I just wanted to thank you again for taking us," I said when she got out of her car. "Gent feels real bad he can't do the things he used to, like driving us over tonight. Maybe it'd be best if nobody mentioned it to him." Keeping my eyes on a fence post behind Mrs. Morales, I was careful to make it sound important, but not important enough to make a big deal over.

Mrs. Morales stood clutching her purse to her side. Finally she said, "Etta May?"

The way she spoke my name, so solemnly, I couldn't help but look at her.

"Did you tell your grandfather I was taking you and Quentin out tonight?"

Biting my lip, I fought to keep away the tears. But this time I couldn't stop them. "Please, Mrs. Morales, *please* don't tell Gent. Quentin had to go to the audition. You said yourself he's got talent. It's just that Quentin has a real hard time in front of people and . . . and he never would've gone without—"

"Your grandfather has a right to know where

you were. No matter why you're keeping it from him—and I'm not saying it's for a bad reason—he's got to know. Now, now. A few tears are good for the soul," she added, putting her arm around me. Even though her purse was wedged into my side, her arm felt comforting. "You want to come in for a while?"

I shook my head. "I'm okay," I said and started for my place.

"You let me know if there's anything you need," called Mrs. Morales. "I'm only a few steps away."

Except for the flickering of the TV screen, the place was dark. Gent had fallen asleep in his chair, his head leaning sideways at an odd angle. I reached down and touched his face before moving his head to rest on the back of the chair.

"Manny?"

"It's just me, Gent."

His eyes opened. "What time is it?"

After I told him, he repeated, "Going on *eleven!*" He sat up in the chair. "Where you been, girl?"

"I already told you, I was at . . ." I stopped, remembering what Mrs. Morales had said. I didn't want him to see my face, so I turned and went into the kitchen. "You want me to get you something to eat?"

"Etta May? You come back here and tell me where you've been all this time."

I came back and even though I stood directly in

front of him, I couldn't look Gent in the eye. "I wasn't at Quentin's the whole time," I started. "Quentin and me were with Mrs. Morales." And then real quiet, I added, "At the auditions." I wasn't certain if he'd heard because he sat in that chair stone silent. I looked up and saw the hurt in his eyes.

Burying my face in his shoulder where the bone cut a line across his shirt, I mumbled, "I didn't mean to lie to you."

After a while Gent pushed away my hair, now wet with tears. "Manny always claimed Loomises could be hard to live with. She called it the contrariness in us, doing what we think is right, no matter what." He stopped to take a breath. "'You and Etta May, one of a kind,' she'd say. 'One of a kind.'" Then he grinned at me. "Nobody ever said us Loomises were easy to live with."

I wanted to hug him right then and there with all my might, but he looked so frail and tired, I kissed his cheek instead.

"Etta May?" he drawled, but I was bursting to tell him about tonight.

"You should've seen Quentin up on that stage, Gent. The whole place got real quiet after he started to sing, like he was somebody famous. Maybe you'll come hear him when he sings at the—"

"Now, girl, don't you go pushing it too far."

I smiled at him, and kissed his other cheek before going off to my room. After I got undressed and was about to climb into bed, it hit me: Gent had been trying to *tell* me something, but I was too filled up with Quentin's audition to understand.

I tapped on his bedroom door. "Gent? Can I come in?"

He grunted something about not being decent yet. I paced back and forth in the hall a couple times before he opened the door. He was wearing his crumpled pajama bottoms and a T-shirt. He went over to the bed and sat down.

"You got something to tell me? That's why you were saying all that stuff about us Loomises, isn't it? Is it about Ma?" I asked, knowing full well it wasn't Ma at all. It was about him.

"Folks should be let to die how they want."

"*Die?* What are you talking about? You said yourself there's nothing to worry ov—"

"There *is* nothing to worry over." Gent took my hand for a moment and squeezed it. "I ain't gonna let them cut me up, like they did Manny." Then he lay down with his back to me.

I covered Gent up with a quilt and went back to my room, where I bawled my heart out.

Chapter Twelve

"Gent's not going to die," I told Ma on the phone later that night. I'd waited to call her until Gent's wheezing had settled down some. *"I won't let him."* It came out with such fierceness that Ma suddenly turned silent. I knew then that something was wrong.

"I tried to tell Pop that you needed to be told." She spoke barely above a whisper and I had to hold the phone tight against my ear to hear her. "But he wanted to be the one to tell you himself in his own time. Insisted even. 'Don't you take that away from a dying man,' he said." She took a deep breath. "Look, I'm not waiting for Saturday. I'm driving down tonight."

"Why can't they *do* something?"

"I wish there was a cure. But there isn't. Oh, baby, please hang in there. I'll be back as soon as I can."

I didn't know if I could hang in there till she came. Just thinking of Gent got me all choked up inside.

The next morning I tried to pretend everything was the same as before—before I knew. It seemed funny, knowing something was true down deep, but not facing up to it. Lord, I still didn't want to. Gent and I bumped into each other as I hurried about in the kitchen. "Ma's on her way," I said as he counted out five teaspoons of coffee grounds into the metal basket. "She'll probably get here by noon." Before he had a chance to question me, I added, "I talked with her last night, after you'd gone to bed."

To keep from crying again, I concentrated on turning the eggs over without breaking them. "Eggs are done the way you like them," I said and slid two on a plate, while I cooked mine longer. Gent liked his on the runny side. "Did you hear that?" I asked, nodding toward the radio that sat on the counter beside the stove. "It's not supposed to rain for another week or so. Guess I'd better water the roses when I get back." Talking about things that were safe, like the weather or his roses, was easier than talking about what was really on my mind.

"No need to," said Gent. "Right leg is stiffer than a brand-new pair of work boots. It's gonna rain.

Yessir, it's gonna rain." His breath came in hard bursts between the words; I wondered each time if he had the strength to draw in another.

"Well, then, I'd better get the pails." I went out to the stoop, grabbed the two plastic pails, and left them under the leaky spots. Gent was good at predicting the rain but not at remembering to get the pails out in time.

When I sat down to eat my breakfast, I noticed Gent was picking at his food. I decided it was no use asking if I could stay home, so after I finished eating I grabbed my books and kissed him good-bye.

Quentin was outside calling my name. "Hurry up," he said as I dragged myself down from the stoop. "Or we're gonna be . . ." Pausing, he looked into my face. "What's wrong, Etta May?"

The words I'd been holding back poured out of me. "Gent's dying. Ma told me over the phone last night."

Quentin came up to me then and put his hand on my shoulder. His touch was soft as a drop of dew. He just stood there with his head bowed and his hand on me, making tiny circles in the dirt road with the heel of his right boot. Finally he looked up. In the corner of his eye I saw a tear.

I was glad I had Quentin to help me make it all the way to three o'clock when the bus drove us home. Soon as we got to our road I saw Ma's car. "Ma's back!" I cried. Instead of the Volkswagen she had driven down in the last time, her Plymouth was parked out front with a U-Haul hitched to the back end. That had to mean Ma was moving in.

I got so excited over her living with Gent and me that I ran up the three steps, calling over my shoulder, "See you later, Quentin."

Inside, I grabbed the pails I had left this morning and took them back out to the stoop. "Doesn't look like it's going to rain after all," I told Gent, who was sitting in his chair by the window. Lord knows why something dumb like that popped out of my mouth. Who cared if Gent's right leg didn't predict it right this time? Ma was back for good. Everything had to get better now.

"Where's Ma?" I started to ask when I heard the door to the bathroom open. Ma stepped out.

"Etta May, honey."

When she put her arms around me I hugged her back. Ma wasn't wearing any makeup, not even lipstick. I'd never known her to go anywhere without it.

"Traffic on the Interstate was tied up several miles," Ma said. "Or I would have been here sooner." She looked tired.

"Want a glass of soda?" I asked.

She nodded and started rummaging around inside her shoulder bag.

"Look at me searching for a cigarette I don't have," she said. "It's automatic, like taking a breath. Crazy, isn't it, how a little thing like that can control your life?" She closed her bag. "I went cold turkey last Friday. Haven't touched a one, not that I haven't thought about it at least a million times . . ."

I took two bottles of root beer out of the refrigerator and filled three glasses. After handing Ma a glass, I took one over to Gent, who had been sitting quietly in his chair the whole time. I noticed him eyeing Ma. "I don't know, Claire . . . I just don't know," he said, shaking his head.

"I'm only doing what's right for you and Etta May, Pop. And for me too. You have to be reasonable about this."

What had they been talking about before I got home? "There's plenty of room," I blurted out. "I'll sleep out here on the couch. I don't mind, honest. And then you can use my . . ." I stopped when I noticed Ma looking at me funny. "The U-Haul out front. Aren't you moving your stuff in?"

"Oh, honey, no, I'm not. I'm sorry you thought that. You and Pop must know you just can't stay here any longer." She stopped. "There's nothing to hold you here anymore, nothing but this broken-down trailer. Moving in with me is the only reasonable thing to do."

"No," I said, shaking my head. "You can't do that. Gent and me are staying *right here*." I went out the door, slamming it behind me.

"Etta May!" called Ma.

Even though I heard her clatter down the steps after me, I kept going. I knew in my heart I wasn't being fair. But if Ma got her way, Gent would give up and die a lot sooner, like Manny did. I wasn't about to let him go just yet.

"Don't you close up on me too, Etta May," Ma called, hurrying down the road after me. "I'm sorry we can't stay here like you and Pop want, but it just isn't possible." She grabbed me by the arm.

When I swung around to face her, I saw Gent looking out the front window.

"Tell me why you don't want to come back with me."

I didn't say anything.

"What *is* it?" she asked, her eyes pleading with me. "Don't clam up on me now."

"*You don't really care,*" I screamed. "This is our home, Gent's and mine. And when the time comes this is where he wants to die." How could I tell her what I felt? That Gent and Manny were the only family I'd ever known. And Quentin was my only true friend. How could I say that to me she was just someone who came to visit every so often, pretending to be my ma? And I pretended to be her daughter.

She let go of my arm. We stood there looking at each other for a moment till finally she said, "I haven't had a bite to eat since I don't know when. Why don't I go pick up some pizza? Then we'll talk this over together calmly, you and me and Pop."

"What's there to talk about?" My voice echoed above the roar of an eighteen-wheeler speeding along the main highway. "You've already made up your mind."

"Look, we'll talk some more when I get back. You want extra pepperoni and cheese on yours?" When I didn't answer, she added, "I'll be back in a jiffy." She walked to her car and drove away, with the U-Haul rattling along behind.

It didn't matter how many reasons Ma had for taking us away from here; I had made Gent a promise. And I wasn't about to go back on it now.

Chapter Thirteen

When I got back to the trailer, Gent was wiping up the kitchen counter. He looked over at me. "Where's your ma?"

"She went to get some pizza."

He nodded, turned away, and rinsed the sponge in the sink. Then he took out three plates and set them on the counter. I got out the forks and paper towels. Gent and I figured paper towels worked just as well as napkins, and we didn't want the extra expense of buying both.

"It's not that your ma's wrong," said Gent, picking up the coffee can from the refrigerator shelf and pulling off the plastic lid. "She's only doing what's practical." He spoke at the can while spooning out the coffee, as if I wasn't there at all.

"Once, when your ma was this high," began Gent, and he raised his hand to just above his knee level, "the three of us drove all the way to

Maine. Manny said she wanted to see some of the U S of A before she got too old and feeble to give a hoot's holler over what she'd missed." Gent put the coffeepot on the stove burner. "We found this pretty lake below a mountain ridge. Got a funny Indian name to it." He thought a moment before shaking his head. "Anyway, we rented a cabin there and stayed four days."

"Four days . . . four *whole* days?" I asked and turned the flame under the coffeepot up. I'd never known him to stay away from home that long.

Gent turned the flame down to where he first had it, all the while muttering about certain people who take over when it isn't asked for. "You hear me tell you it was three-and-a-quarter days, girl?" But I knew he was teasing because he winked at me.

"You saying we should pack up and go with Ma? After all the times you've told me, 'When the time comes, Etta May, you let me die at home in my own bed.' Don't deny those are your exact words."

Gent slowly settled on a stool, pointing his elbows into the countertop. His thin shoulders raised with each breath, and I heard the familiar wheezing. "I ain't denying anything. But you listen here, girl." Gent started coughing so hard I thought he was going to choke. I brought him a glass of water. But he waved it away and instead took a tissue from his back pocket and wiped his mouth. "A man's got to do what a man's got to do," he said in a raspy voice. "You understand? Don't you give your ma a hard time on this, neither."

When I opened my mouth to speak, Gent held up his hand. "It's only right for you to be together. You're going to need her much as she needs you. And I don't want to hear any back talk."

"What about you, Gent? You didn't exactly say you were coming too."

"You hear anything to the contrary?"

"No." But from the way he looked, tired and drawn into himself, I had an uneasy feeling.

After Ma got back, we sat in the kitchen eating the pizza, though Gent mostly nibbled on the crust and sipped coffee. When she realized Gent and I weren't putting up a fuss, Ma started talking about how good it was going to be with the three of us living together.

"What about Eddie?" I blurted out.

Ma's face frosted over. "What does Eddie have to do with our conversation?"

I shrugged and kept my mouth shut.

After a few seconds of silence, Ma said, "I'm glad the two of you decided it's better this way." She leaned over and put one hand on mine and the other on Gent's. "We'll be okay. I know we will," she added, looking at Gent. "There's a park down the street from where I live, Pop. It's got lots of benches and a baseball diamond where the neighbor kids go. Remember when you'd take me to Bergman Ball Park to watch the local leagues and we'd find the highest spot in the stands? I thought I was sitting on top of the world. Back then those stands seemed to touch the sky. I suppose they were probably no more than six feet off the ground."

"You really think he cares about sitting on a park bench all day or watching a bunch of kids play baseball? What about his roses? He won't have his roses to work on anymore."

"I know that!" she snapped. "We'll get some flower boxes to put around the apartment windows. It could use a little brightening up anyway. Pop can keep them filled with—"

"Flower boxes," I muttered. "Are you kidding?"

"That's enough, Etta May." Ma locked eyes with me.

The stool Gent was sitting on scratched against the tile floor. Silently he shuffled into the hallway and disappeared into his bedroom. I realized then what a terrible thing we had just done, talking about Gent right in front of him, as if he had no understanding or feeling.

"It's settled. Despite what you might think." Ma sighed. "Here I thought Pop would be the hard one to persuade."

I decided to let that pass.

"It's not going to be as bad as you think. You'll be close to school. Only two blocks away is Woodrow Wilson Junior High, where Ruthie Myerson goes. She must be your age, or close to it. Nice kid. She lives down the hall from—"

"We got some chocolate ice cream left. You want any?" I didn't want to hear another word about Ruthie what's-her-face or Woodrow Wilson Junior High.

After I helped Ma finish cleaning up, I went to get my jacket. "I'm going over to Quentin's for a while," I called, letting the door slam behind me. I didn't know how I was going to tell him I was moving. Maybe if I broke it slow, I thought. I knocked only twice, and the door flew open. Quentin pulled me in.

"You trying to yank off my arm or something?"

Quentin started hopping around the living room like a jackrabbit on a hot griddle. "I got news, Etta May," he sang out.

"How am I supposed to talk to a . . . News?"

Quentin now stood in the middle of the room with a grin so wide it practically split his face in two.

"You telling me you got the call?"

He nodded.

"When?"

"Just before Pa left for work tonight. The man said I had a real nice voice."

I let out a hoot and grabbed Quentin's hands. Together we danced around the living room till the whole place rattled. Finally, we collapsed on the floor. "And now, ladies and gentlemen," I said, getting back up on my feet. "Straight from Liberty where his songs have blasted right off the music charts, may I present country music's newest and hottest star. The one, the only, *Quentin . . . Oaks.*" Holding out my hand, I said, "Take it away!"

Shrugging, Quentin didn't budge from the floor.

"Get up," I said, giving him a boot on the behind. "Can't you pretend?" When he finally did get up, I clapped till my hands stung. "Take a bow."

"But I haven't done anything yet."

"You bow when the audience—that's me if you didn't know—claps."

"I don't bow good."

"You don't need to bow good, just move your head up and down once or twice, like this." I waited for Quentin to try it. "See? That's not so bad. When you think about it, neither was getting up on the stage."

He looked at me a moment, slowly shaking his

head and grinning at the same time. "They got a band, and I'm to practice with them tomorrow. My turn is from two-thirty to three. Pa's going to drive me over. You'll come, won't you, Etta May? I can't sing without you there."

"You listen here, Quentin Oaks, you don't need me or anybody else around for you to sing good."

Quentin's grin melted away. "What are you talking about?"

"I'm saying . . ." I took a deep breath. "I'm saying nobody—not me, not your pa, not even your mama—can do it for you." I bit my lip till it hurt. "I'm saying that Gent and me are starting to pack up tomorrow because we're going back with my ma to live."

Quentin blinked twice.

I wasn't sure it had sunk in, so I added, "I wish more than anything I could go with you. *And* to the Jamboree. But Ma wants to leave by the first of next week so she doesn't lose any more time off from work."

"You telling me I won't ever see you again, Etta May?" Quentin's words, soft and light as dust, hung in the air.

I looked at him standing in front of me, hands shoved in his jeans pockets and looking sad, and I got all choked up inside. It was no use telling him I'd come back, because Quentin was smart enough to know it probably would never happen.

Chapter Fourteen

ᕙᕗ ᕙᕗ ᕙᕗ ᕙᕗ ᕙᕗ ᕙᕗ

When I got back later from Quentin's, I found Gent outside standing by Summer Song. He looked up at me. "Always do my best thinking here." Shadows cut across his face, smoothing out the tired lines.

I pulled a blade of grass and poked the tip into my mouth. "Thinking about what?"

He shrugged. "Different things. Look, here, girl," he said, pointing at a bud. "So early on in the growing season and Summer Song's about to bloom."

I smiled. "Must be from all the extra special attention it's been getting." Looking past him, I saw that Ma's car was gone. "Where'd Ma go?"

"To see Bill Spinelli. Seems to think he'll buy the place back. Said she'd even sweeten the deal by throwing in the pickup. Didn't ask if it was all right by me. Nope, not one word." Gent started for the toolshed with me trailing close behind. "If she had, I would've told her that crafty ol' coot won't be happy. No siree. Not till he's got the whole dang lot for near nothin'." The hiss from Gent trying to suck in as much air as he could filled the tiny shed. "He's seeing money signs all over Claire right now."

I almost let slip that neither the trailer nor his pickup was a bargain and we'd be lucky to get them off our hands.

After hanging up his hoe, Gent turned to face me and I saw a devilish look in his eye. Then he took off, shuffling to the end of the driveway, where he climbed into the pickup. "What are you waiting for, girl?" he called out the window. "We got business to tend to."

Gent didn't say what he was up to, and I figured it was no use asking, but I got the gist when he turned off the main road toward Mr. Spinelli's place. Parked in front of the big frame house was Ma's Plymouth, with the U-Haul still attached.

From the screen door I saw Ma and Mr. Spinelli sitting opposite each other in the living room. Gent banged on the screen.

"Pop! What are you doing here?" Ma said before turning to me. "Etta May, you know better than to—"

"Quiet, Claire. Bill and me got business to discuss."

Mr. Spinelli made a clucking sound. "I've known you thirty years or more, Dan," he said. "And in all that time you hardly ever began a conversation with a neighborly greeting. Right to the point; that's you, Dan, right to the point. But you've wasted your time coming down. Claire and me have already come to an agreem—"

"You see me sign any papers?" huffed Gent. "How much are you putting up?"

Ma answered. "Mr. Spinelli has agreed to take the place off our hands, Pop, even your pickup." Her eyes pleaded with Gent to leave matters alone.

"For practically nothing. That's what you're trying to tell me. I wasn't born yesterday, Claire. They're worth at least four thousand. You can't tell me they ain't."

"Look here, Dan, I'm doing you and your family a favor by taking on something that won't be easy to—"

"Forty-five hundred seems about right," said Gent, leaning toward Mr. Spinelli and shoving his knobby finger into Mr. Spinelli's shoulder. "If I remember right, those two lots you've been fillin' up out back are wetlands. Ain't there a law against that?"

Mr. Spinelli's face turned red.

"You make the check out in Claire's name and

send the papers home with her so I can sign 'em." Gent went over to the doorway and, tipping his cap, shoved open the screen door with his other hand.

As I followed Gent back to the pickup, I could see Ma still standing there with her jaw hanging open. "You sure pulled one on Mr. Spinelli," I said as the pickup lurched into gear. At the crossroads, instead of taking a right, Gent turned left. "Aren't we going home?"

"Got some more business to take care of first." Gent drove toward Liberty till he got to Cemetery Hill. On the north side was Manny's grave. As he turned off the ignition, Gent threw his hand over his chest. His back straightened and I could see he was having an extra hard time catching his breath.

I moved toward him. *"Gent!"*

"I'm all right," he said, waving me away. "Just a little pain." After a while, he sat up and swung the door open.

"You stay here," he ordered when I started to climb out. I got back in and watched him slowly walk the short distance to the side of the hill where Manny lay buried beneath a double stone. The names and birthdates of Emmanuelle and Daniel Loomis had been chiseled into it. Only Manny's side had the date of death.

Gent stood there a long time with his cap in his hands and his head bent.

*   *   *

From the other side of my bedroom wall I could hear the squeak of Gent's bedsprings. I got up to go to the bathroom and on my way back I saw a sliver of light from below his door creeping out into the hallway.

"Gent?" I called softly. "You okay?"

He opened the door and stood beside it, his shoulders drawn together. Seeing him like that made me think of a butterfly with its wings folded up.

"I can't sleep either," I said.

Then I noticed he was hugging something to him. When I took a step closer I saw what it was: a photo of Manny, slender and young.

On the bed lay the thick photo album Gent and I used to look at together. It was so long ago, I'd almost forgotten. Maybe it was the way I was staring at the album now, but Gent took my hand. "Remember, girl?" he said, gently drawing me inside.

"I remember."

Gent nodded, and we sat on the edge of his bed.

Before opening up the album, I rubbed my hand over its worn leather cover. Inside, I paused by each picture so Gent could match faces with as many names as he could come up with. "Memory ain't what it used to be," he said, tapping his fingernail over a photo so old it was different shades of brown and curled at the edges. "Can't put a name to that face. But Manny, she'd tell us who . . ." His voice faded away till only the sound of his wheezing filled the tiny room.

"What are you two doing up at this hour of the night?" Ma stood by the door clutching her thin blue robe to her. Long strands of hair fell over her face and she swept them away with the back of her hand.

"Look, here's that one of you, Ma, when you were my age," I said. Funny how me calling her Ma to her face slipped out. It wasn't something I often did, and I wondered if she noticed.

She sat down on the other side of Gent, who had moved to make room for her. She laughed kind of girlishly when she saw what I was pointing at. In the picture Ma stood next to a big maple tree, her head thrown back in laughter. On that same tree, swinging from a tire that hung on a rope, was a dark-haired boy.

"Poor Willie," said Ma. "Right after that picture was taken he started showing off. Guess he thought swinging upside down on that tire would impress me. The next thing I knew he landed on his behind right in front of me." She giggled. "I'm not sure what hurt more, his sore bottom or his embarrassment."

"Willie," I said, remembering the name. "You mean Willie Carter? The one you and Gent were talking about when we were driving over to that doctor?"

"You remembered his name?"

At the time I wondered if Willie could be my pa. "Why not?" I said aloud. "The way you were talking about him, I thought maybe you kind of liked him back. Did you and Willie ever date?"

Ma gave me a sly look, as if she was catching on to what I trying to ask. But before I could say another word, she changed the subject. "Look, Pop, there's you and Mama right after you were married."

Manny, wearing a wide-brimmed hat and lacy dress, and Gent, in a dark jacket and pants, stood on the front steps of the parsonage. Manny was looking into the camera, but Gent wasn't. He had his eyes fastened on Manny and his arm around her waist.

"We didn't wait for no big church wedding. We just decided it was time." Gent drew up his shoulders. "Got everything done a few days before. License, blood test, and rounding up the preacher. Forty-six years we had, Manny and me, good years too. I'm not saying they weren't without troubles, but they were good years." Gent looked over at Ma. "Nineteen of them before you were even born. We'd given up hope." He took her hand. "Manny always said, 'The Good Lord has His own timepiece.'"

"You and Mama," began Ma, her voice quivery. "You deserved a daughter who would've—"

"No," he said sharply.

I looked over at Ma and saw her eyes wet with tears.

Gent took my hand into his and I was no longer afraid. We held on tight, the three of us. And for the first time, we were family.

Chapter Fifteen

When I awoke the next morning, I heard Ma and Gent's voices in the kitchen. I got up and padded down the hallway.

"You don't have to worry about a thing, Pop. I already called his office. It's all set," said Ma.

"I ain't going to no hospital." Gent looked as though he was about to slap his hand on the counter, to make a bigger point. But instead, he threw it over his chest like he had done at the cemetery. Ma, her back to him, never noticed. I was ready to go to him if he needed help, but whatever it was soon passed.

"All I said was, Dr. Kelsy is sending on your medical records to this clinic near me."

"Didn't you hear me, Claire?" Gent sputtered in a raspy voice. "I ain't going to no hospital."

Ma sighed and when she finally spoke I knew she had had enough of Gent's talk. "It's a *clinic,*

Pop. Just a clinic, where you can get some help when you need it. That's all." Ma turned then and saw me standing near the doorway. "I'm scrambling up some eggs. Can you help with the toast?"

Nodding, I went over to the breadbox and pulled out a loaf of bread. Spreading four slices on a cookie sheet, I put it in the broiler section of the oven. Ever since our toaster broke down, I'd been using the oven.

Except for the sound of his wheezing, Gent was silent, his head bowed as though in prayer. He got up and began to shuffle toward the bathroom.

"Pop, aren't you having something to eat?"

He shook his head.

As he passed me, I wanted to put my arms around him and tell him everything would be all right. Even though there was nothing I could do about us moving away, I was going to keep my promise to him. One way or another.

Ma stirred the eggs and poured them into a pan. "I just don't know how I could've done it any different." She said it quietly, more to herself than to me.

"Ma . . . I was wondering." I took the cookie sheet out of the oven and began turning each slice over to brown the other side. "We're taking some of the big things with us, aren't we? You know, like Gent's bed?" Then I slid the cookie sheet back under the broiler for another half a minute.

"You and I will share my double bed, at least till I can afford a bigger apartment. As for Pop, I already have a rollaway set up in a corner of the living room. And besides, by the time we pack up everything else I don't think we'll have room for a—"

"We have to *make* room. It's what he's used to. You know he can't sleep on a bed he's not used to." I stopped talking because the sound of Gent's hacking cough filtered down the hallway into the kitchen.

Ma looked past the doorway into the hall. "We'll see," she whispered. "We'll see."

After breakfast Ma and I went out to the U-Haul to get the empty boxes she had picked up at the drugstore. Together we hauled them into the trailer and began separating the things we'd take from things that would go to the Salvation Army.

"Why can't we just leave what we don't want right here?"

She eyed me for a moment before handing me one of the bigger boxes. "You might as well start over there," she said, nodding toward the cabinets.

Gent, hearing all the racket, wandered into the kitchen. He didn't say anything, just sat on a stool, looking tired and sad, as Ma and I filled the boxes. I noticed his eyes flash when Ma was about to put a chipped serving dish into the Salvation Army box. Gent grabbed it out of her hands. "This ain't going to no stranger," he mumbled, and put it in the box to go back with us. "You take the rest of them dishes in that cupboard too."

"Pop, I got all the dishes I need already."

Gent lifted a wiry brow.

"Oh, all right," said Ma, "but we got only so much room. If you and Etta May keep insisting on taking things we don't need, we could end up with the U-Haul and car all packed up and no place for the two of you to sit. But I suppose," Ma added, looking us over, "neither of you would mind if you were left behind."

"Won't do a bit of good supposin', now will it, Claire?" The corners of Gent's eyes crinkled up and for an instant I noticed a grin on his grizzly face.

By late afternoon Ma and I and Gent, who had been hanging around directing traffic, had filled six large boxes with clothes, the broken-down toaster, two radios that picked up more static than anything else, and some old tools Ma finally talked Gent into letting go. Then Ma and I dragged the boxes out to the U-Haul so she could take them to the Salvation Army.

"Go with your ma," Gent called from the stoop. Before turning to go back inside, he muttered, "Ain't been any peace and quiet around here all day."

"If it's peace and quiet you want, Pop," Ma called back, laughing, "then you'd better figure on only an hour of it 'cause Etta May and I'll be back to stir things up some more."

It was slow going to the Salvation Army and back, since Ma was worried about towing the trailer. "Will you hand me a tissue?" asked Ma. "There's a box in the glove compartment."

When I took out a tissue, I noticed something curled up behind the box. "What's this?" I asked, pulling out a catalog.

"I've started taking night classes at this junior college where I live. When Mama passed away it hit me. I was barely making it from day to day, and now I had more than just myself to consider. When you're young, Etta May, you think you got your whole life ahead and the world will turn over for you. But it doesn't happen that way." She shook her head. "No, it just doesn't happen that way."

I looked at Ma and wondered what she meant. She didn't mention Gent and me, but I had a feeling we were what she was talking about.

Country music played softly on the radio. As I

listened, I thought of Quentin and wondered how he'd done at the rehearsal. "Quentin's been chosen to sing at WHUG's Jumpin' Jamboree in two weeks. I'm not one bit surprised he was picked, because he's got a voice smoother than silk. If only I could go too." I paused a bit. "Quentin doesn't like to sing in front of strangers. He *needs* me there."

"I wish we could all be there, you and me and Pop," Ma said, keeping her eyes on the road.

I don't know what it was that made me say what I said next.

"I've been thinking about . . . about my . . ." I didn't want her to get her dander up like she always did when I'd mention something she didn't want to talk about, but I couldn't stop now. "About my pa. Gent and Manny and you—nobody'll talk about him. Tell me, Ma, *please*," I begged, "tell me who he is."

After a long moment, she said, "Guess I have a knack for picking the wrong guy. Like your father . . . and Eddie, though this time I came to my senses before it was too late." Ma took a deep breath and held it before slowly letting it out.

"I was crazy, wild, back then. I was only sixteen when Jimmy Tucker rode into my life on that flaming red Harley Davidson of his." Ma looked as if she could see it now. "One month of sneaking out almost every night and riding with my arms fastened to his waist, and feeling like . . . oh, I don't know, like I was grown up for the first time in my life. Pop was furious. I'd never seen him so mad the night he caught me climbing out my bedroom window. But you know, when Jimmy Tucker rode off in his fringed leather jacket for the very last time, I knew I was lucky to be rid of him."

I couldn't believe she had finally told me. She glanced over at me and our eyes met. "I didn't find out I was having you until a few weeks later. I never told Jimmy. I'm sorry, baby. I'm sorry I can't give you a real father. All I have is an old picture and the name of his hometown, but I don't know if he lives there anymore. He told me he came from a big family, though, and I suppose some of them are still around."

I nodded and thought someday I'd look him up. But for now I had more questions, and since Ma seemed to be in a talkative mood, I decided this was as good a time as any to ask them. "What about Eddie?"

"Eddie," Ma repeated his name. "I hated it when Mama and Pop kept secrets from me, and here I've been doing the same to you. I wanted Eddie and you and me and Pop to be a family. But Eddie didn't see it that way. He was the emergency that took me away, only now I know I never should have left you and Pop. Eddie's gone; this time for good."

Even though we were almost home, she pulled off to the side of the road and turned to face me. "Oh, baby," she whispered, "I know I've hurt you. I didn't plan on leaving the way I did. It just happened."

A tear slipped down my cheek and Ma brushed it aside with her thumb.

"I can tell you the same reasons I told myself, reasons to help me live with what I'd done. I'd just turned seventeen. I was worried sick over what I was going to do with this tiny new person. But I couldn't give you up to a stranger, so I left you with Mama and Pop. Just for a while, I told myself, just time enough to get away from here when I still had a chance, and when I made it on my own I'd come back for you. I never planned for it to happen like it did." Ma shook her head. "I don't know the answer, I only know that now I want to make it right."

The rest of what she was saying became lost in the wail of an ambulance as it shot past us in the opposite lane. "Didn't that just pull out of our road?" I asked, my heart thumping back and forth like a Ping-Pong ball.

Chapter Sixteen

Neither Ma or I spoke as we pulled into our drive. Out front stood Mrs. Morales and three other neighbors. We were getting out of the car when Mrs. Morales came over and threw her arms around me.

"They just took Dan away," she said.

"No, no!" I screamed, backing away. "He *can't* go to the hospital. *He can't!*"

"He begged not to go," said Mrs. Morales. "But what could we do? With him so sick, what could we do? I found him lying right there." She pointed to a spot in front of Summer Song.

"That's fine. There was nothing else anyone could've done," said Ma, before excusing herself and going into the trailer. When she returned she was holding Gent's spare key ring.

It was seven miles to Liberty and Ma drove as fast as she could. I felt the sway of the truck bed and heard the exhaust pipe thumping along the road to a silent beat. I concentrated on the thump-thump-thump, trying desperately to keep away the scary thoughts.

It's funny how much alike Ma and I were about some things. Like when we're worrying, we clam up. Manny was different; when she got worked up, she would talk your ear off. She said Ma and I took after Gent that way. Then she'd laugh that fluttery little laugh and say, "Must be in his genes." For a long time, whenever I heard her say that, I thought she was talking about *jeans,* and I wondered what Gent's baggy old jeans had to do with Ma and me.

"Remind me to call Pastor Duncan and let him know Pop's in the hospital," said Ma, breaking into my thoughts.

"What for? What good did all his praying over Manny do?"

Ma sighed. "Mama never missed a Sunday if she could help it. And sometimes she got Pop to go too. What good did it do? The last time I saw Mama, I knew she'd found what she'd been seeking. I just didn't know what it was." Ma's voice turned quiet. "Maybe it's different for everybody."

The most I spoke after that was, "Can't this go any faster?" Considering we were in the pickup,

Ma made pretty good time. She drove the seven miles in fifteen minutes flat. When she couldn't find a space in the nearby parking lot, she let me off by the emergency door. I scrambled inside and over to a glassed-in cubicle, where a woman in a green stretch jumper sat. "I'm looking for my grandfather," I blurted out. "He came in on an ambulance." When she wrinkled her brow, I added, "Daniel Loomis?"

"Oh, that one. I was just getting the file up on the computer." She looked at the screen. "Ah, yes, here it is. Is his address still Postal Box 26, Sunshine Pines Trailer Court, North—"

"*Yes.* When can I see him?"

"I just need to verify a little more information, then you may see Mr. Loomis."

"You don't need to verify anything because he's not staying long enough for it to matter."

Ma came up from behind. "What's going on, Etta May?"

The woman in the green jumper gave a little cough. "I have Mr. Loomis's admission papers right here and they've already been signed by his regular physician, Dr. Kelsy."

"We're taking Gent back home with us. Tell her, Ma. Tell her we're taking him home."

Ma sighed. "Don't you understand how sick Pop is? I'm sorry, honey, but I can't think of any other way. He needs special care, something you and I can't give him."

"No," I said, raising my voice, "*you* don't understand. He wants to die at home, not here all hooked up like Manny did, but at home in his own bed. I gave him my word and I mean to keep it."

Ma, taking hold of my arm, spoke low. "Don't you make a scene. We have to keep our heads. For Pop's sake." When I didn't answer, she said, "Etta May?"

I bit my lip to keep quiet.

While Ma gave Green Jumper the information, I leaned against a wall and stared at the white coats moving in and out of the double doors. The worst hadn't happened, I decided, or they would have told us. Maybe it wasn't as bad as Ma and I thought, and Gent wouldn't have to stay long.

"Go through there and take a left," said Green Jumper, nodding toward the double doors. "Mr. Loomis is in room four." As we were leaving, she added, "I hope your grandfather can go home soon."

We found Gent in a small room. The other two beds were empty, and the curtains between the beds were only half drawn. I brushed my lips across his sunken cheek. He seemed lost in the bed; tiny, and lost and older than I'd remembered.

"Gent," I said, "couldn't you come up with a better plan to keep you and me from going off to Pittsburgh?"

He didn't say anything, just made a lopsided grin. Then he reached out with both hands to Ma and me, and I noticed how shaky he was. All the while his eyes kept probing me with questions I couldn't answer.

A nurse came into the room. "Mr. Loomis," she said, "Dr. Kelsy has scheduled you for some tests." The nurse and an aide who was with her stepped up to the bed, while Ma and I backed away.

"Tests?" Gent's bushy brows pinched together.

"This must be your family," said the aide in a cheery voice as she tucked in his sheets. The nurse took the chart she was holding and laid it at the foot of Gent's bed.

"What tests?" he demanded, his voice low and gravelly as he paused to suck air into his lungs.

The nurse smiled. "Just a few X rays and some blood tests." In no time they rolled his bed out the doorway and were heading straight for an elevator across the hall. "Mr. Loomis will be assigned a room on the third floor," the nurse added, turning around to tell Ma and me as we trailed along behind. "You might want to check at the nurses' station on 3B in about an hour or so." The elevator doors opened and he was whisked inside.

"I don't need no—" I heard Gent say before the closing doors cut off his voice.

Ma and I ended up in the hospital snack bar sitting across from each other. I was finishing up a Coke while Ma stared into her coffee cup and fidgeted with her hair, tugging and pulling a few strands. Then she blurted out, "I think I'll get some fresh air." We got up and Ma paid the fat lady sitting on a stool beside the register. Out in the hall as we were passing by a tiny gift shop, Ma elbowed me. "Why don't you pick out something for yourself?" she said, handing me a five-dollar bill. "I'll be out on the front terrace. Take your time."

Buying something for me while Gent was in the hospital didn't seem right, so I shook my head.

"Oh, honey, all of this has been such a worry on you." When I still refused to take the money, Ma shoved it into my hand and, giving me a gentle nudge toward the shop, added, "I want you to find something nice for yourself."

Maybe Ma wanted to be alone, I decided, wandering inside and over to the counter. My eyes settled on a dancing bear in a music box. When the woman behind the counter saw me staring, she wound it up and the bear, wearing a pink tutu, began to dance daintily on one furry leg round and round in tiny circles. Watching the silly-looking bear kept my mind off Gent for a moment. Then, moving along the shelf of gifts displayed in two neat rows, I noticed a black velvet stand. Attached to it were different animal-shaped pins.

I took down the ladybug.

The first time I saw a real ladybug was when I was no more than five. I was outside playing near Gent when I spotted it, and knowing how he squashed any bug he found near his roses, I steadied my foot over it. But Gent, who was pulling weeds at the time, said just as cool as you please, "If it's bad luck you're lookin' for, girl, go ahead an' kill the little critter." Of course that stopped me from squashing it right then and there. Gent put his hand beside the blade of grass and it crawled onto his thumb. "This here's a ladybug an' they bring good luck." He raised his arm and I watched as the ladybug flew away. "You remember that, Etta May," he had said.

When I walked out to the front terrace I had thirty-eight cents in change and the ladybug pinned to my blouse. I found Ma sitting alone with her back to me on a concrete bench, puffing on a cigarette. Seeing her smoking again made my face hot. Her word wasn't worth a hill of beans. I walked up quietly behind her till a branch snapped. She jumped up clear off that bench so fast I thought she was going to take off like a jet.

"For Pete's sake, Etta May. You shouldn't sneak up on a person like that."

"You told Gent and me you'd quit. 'Cold turkey,' you said. But you'll keep right on smoking till you end up with cancer, like Manny."

"I did quit. But then I guess I started again. I'm *trying* to quit!"

"I'll bet," I said, but Ma chose to ignore that as she crushed the cigarette into the grass with the bottom of her shoe. I looked at my watch. "It's been almost an hour. I'm going to check on Gent now."

"Okay, honey, I'll be up soon."

At the third-floor nurses' station a phone was ringing, but nobody was there to answer it. I looked around and that's when I heard voices coming from a nearby room. I wandered over and peered inside. A sign over the bed where three nurses huddled read OXYGEN: NO SMOKING. One of them was speaking to the person on the bed. "You need to calm yourself. Mrs. James was only following doctor's orders. An IV, that's all it is, just a tube to put fluids into your body. Now, with your cooperation we can finish up here and go on to our other patients." I noticed a needle in her hand. She moved aside then, and I was able to get a better look.

"Gent," I yelled, pushing my way over to him.

He was red-faced and wheezing so hard I thought he'd bust a gut. "Leave my grandfather alone. He doesn't want anything." Tears poured out of me. "*Please*, just leave him alone."

I felt a hand brush against my arm. "We're not here to upset you or your grandfather. I'll tell you what. Dr. Kelsy will be making his rounds later this afternoon and Mr. Loomis can speak to him then about procedures." Soon the squish of their soft shoes on the tile floor dissolved into the hallway.

Remembering the pin, I took it off and attached it to Gent's hospital gown. "Ladybug luck," I whispered.

"Told them I don't want nothin' but a shot," he sputtered. "That's all. Nothin' more." Gent started coughing. Finally, he laid his head back and I smoothed out the sheets till I decided he looked more comfortable. "No, sir," he wheezed, "nothin' more."

I pulled up a chair. "Ma mentioned earlier about calling Pastor Duncan. But I don't think she has yet. If you want, I can tell her not to."

"Lord Almighty . . . Manny is still sittin' right here on my conscience. Same as ever. Even got your ma doing her bidding." He started coughing again and I waited. I was surprised when he said, "You let her call, girl."

I looked across the room at the empty bed and

at the partially open locker where Gent's clothes hung. And that gave me an idea. "Gent?" I put my face next to his. "We can break out of here, just you and me," I said, my voice low. "Now's our chance. Ma is still downstairs and nobody's around. The truck's outside and I know you always got your own set of keys on you."

He looked at me for what seemed a long time. Finally he spoke, drawing out his words carefully like they were stretched one after another on a long string. "It's this body, girl. Too old . . . and too tired." He smiled sorrowfully and closed his eyes.

I thought he mumbled something more, so I leaned closer and whispered, "What, Gent?" But all I heard was the familiar rhythmic wheezing as he slept.

Chapter Seventeen

By the time Ma came upstairs I was burning mad over what they would have done to Gent if I hadn't come in time. I told Ma all about it in a low voice so I wouldn't disturb Gent. "We can't let them do that," I said. "We *can't*. If we could just get him h—"

"I wanted you and Pop to go back with me so we could be together, at least while he was still able to get around. But now it looks like it just isn't going to happen." Ma paused and I saw a quiet sadness in her eyes. "Pop's too sick to go."

"No, Ma, you're wrong about Gent."

"I wish I was, honey. But I can promise you one thing. The doctors won't do anything he doesn't want done."

Did Ma really mean it? Would she stick to her promise? Questions kept running through my mind as we waited for Doc Kelsy. At five o'clock

Ma brought up tuna sandwiches and two Cokes from the snack bar and we ate them while Gent picked at his creamed chicken. I could see he was awful uncomfortable, and when the nurse came with his shot he took it eagerly. Soon afterward he fell back asleep. He was snoring up a mighty storm when Doc stuck his head through the doorway and motioned Ma and me out into the hallway.

Doc had bushy hair that matched his white lab-coat and a thick, worried brow. "Dan refused to take the tests or the IV I ordered earlier today. But I'm not really surprised. I've known your father a good long time and he's never been one to keep his opinions to himself."

"He doesn't want to be hooked up to a bunch of machines," I blurted out.

Doc looked over his half-glasses at me.

"My daughter and I support whatever my father wants." Ma slipped her hand over mine and gently squeezed it.

"He has pneumonia. For a patient with emphysema, this is very serious. The tests would only verify that his lungs are badly damaged. I'm sorry you have to face this all over again."

Doc's words floated in my head, and I felt a numbness creeping all through me.

"Maybe with antibiotics we'll be able to prolong Dan's life. But only for a while, till he goes through it all over again." Doc took off his glasses and rubbed the bridge of his nose. "Dan already signed the form not to use extraordinary means when he was admitted. Of course, antibiotics and routine tests aren't considered extraordinary. But if he doesn't want even that, I'm willing to go along with his wishes."

Doc paused and I wondered if telling us came hard for him. Or was it just something he had to do? "Dan won't be able to get out of bed from now on. He's going to need a lot of care, more than you and your daughter can provide. You might want to consider our Extended Care Center, Claire. It's a special facility set up near the hospital. It's not home, but we try to make it feel as homelike as possible. You or your daughter can even stay on a cot in his room. Do you want me to talk with Dan about it?"

Ma nodded, mumbling a thank you.

Doc patted Ma's arm. "We don't want to interrupt the natural end to life for Dan," he said, and went back to Gent's room.

Doc's words drove the truth so deep I was too stunned to move or even cry, and Ma had to nudge me back into reality.

Afterward, in a rasping voice, Gent told us, "Doc and me . . . we got an understanding." He started coughing again, and when I went to help him, a notion popped into my head. It lit up like Fourth of July fireworks, and I knew then how it was with Gent and me, and with Ma too. All those things we wanted. Gent wanting to die peacefully in his own bed. And Ma wanting to do what she thought was best by moving us to Pittsburgh. And me? I guess what I truly wanted was to keep it all from breaking into pieces.

But what you want and what you have to do can be different things entirely. You got to make do with what gets handed to you. "Gent," I whispered, taking his bony hand into mine and pressing it to my face. "You're going to die in your own bed. Just like I promised."

"But Pop already agreed to the Extended Care—"

"I know, Ma," I said, looking up at her. "Tomorrow Quentin and his pa will help us put that U-Haul to good use. Gent, tomorrow we'll move your bed over to the Center." I leaned over and kissed him on the cheek. "Only you got to put up with having Ma and me around, 'cause there's nothing that can be done about that."

Though a tear crawled along a crevice in his cheek, Gent was smiling.

Chapter Eighteen

When we got back from the hospital, I noticed a light on at Mrs. Morales's place. I went over to tell her about Gent and the Extended Care Center.

"You and your mother have more than enough worries without having to cook too," she said when I was about to leave. "The least I can do is lighten that part of your load," and she sent me home with a casserole dish and a strawberry pie still warm from the oven.

I found Quentin and his pa standing inside the opened door with Ma. "Looks like Mrs. Morales is making sure we don't starve," said Ma, taking the casserole and setting it on the counter. I put the pie down beside it.

"Manny and Dan was real special to Quentin and me," began Mr. Oaks, "always looking out for us. Like family. We'd be real honored to help out tomorrow. I'm on second shift so we can move the bed first thing in the morning. Is eight too early?"

"Eight should be fine, but I'll check with the Center first," answered Ma, and she thanked him before I had a chance to do it myself.

"If you folks need anything more done, you be sure to give a holler." Mr. Oaks motioned to the door. "Come on, son. We'd better get on home and leave the ladies alone to—"

"I was about to make a pot of coffee," Ma put in. "Why don't you and Quentin start by helping us with this pie?" It didn't take much persuading to get Mr. Oaks and Quentin over to the kitchen counter.

The whole time we sat eating, Quentin didn't mention one word about the practice session; he mostly concentrated on his share of the strawberry pie. I was bursting to know. Finally, I elbowed him. "How'd practice go?"

His ears turned pink.

There I go again, I thought, and felt bad because I should have known by the way Quentin was acting he didn't want to talk about it.

"You sang fine, son." Mr. Oaks beamed. "Just remember to look up like the man said, so everybody out in the auditorium can hear you better." He looked at Ma and me. "They even asked Quentin if he would sing another song for the show."

"Pa."

Mr. Oaks didn't pay any attention. "Quentin sang this new one—'Ridin' the Rails' it's called—and it's got a beat that makes your feet want to get up and dance around." He threw Quentin a fake right-handed punch before leaning over and ruffling his hair. "Wrote it himself."

"*Pa,*" moaned Quentin.

I noticed Ma then, smiling over the counter at Quentin, her hands cupped around her coffee mug. That's when a thought occurred to me. The whole time we sat there sipping coffee and eating pie, she hadn't once bothered to reach for a smoke.

"When do we get to hear you?" Ma asked.

"Well, now, Quentin would be real glad to sing, wouldn't you, son?"

This time Quentin's face turned a deep red.

"Just a few lines from that new song of—" Before Mr. Oaks could finish, Quentin got up and ran out the door. Mr. Oaks sat there, his face twisted into a big question mark. "What's gotten into that boy?"

"It's probably the jitters from worrying over the show," I said, casual as you please, though my heart was pumping hard just thinking of what Quentin must be feeling right now. Before either Ma or Mr. Oaks could say anything more, I was out the door.

I found Quentin on the front stoop of his trailer,

gazing into the night. "Nothing's the same any-more," he said, without looking up. "Pa and those other people I don't even know expecting things from me." His words drifted along a current of air. "Pa says my singin' is a gift and I should be proud to share it. He's right, I guess. But I won't be sin-gin' for you no more."

"You can't get rid of me that easy," I said. "On the way home tonight I asked Ma if she might look for a job around Liberty—now that we'll be staying as long as Gent is at the Center."

"Is she going to?" asked Quentin, his eyes brightening.

"All she said was, 'We'll see.' But you know me."

Quentin nodded. "Sure do, Etta May, and you don't give up so easy."

I grinned at him.

"Etta May? What if . . . what if you do leave?"

"It won't happen. And even if it did—and that's not saying it will—I wouldn't let you forget me. Not ever. I'd hound you till your dying day. That's a promise." I settled down beside Quentin and thought of Ma and how she was now part of my life almost as much as Gent was. And Quentin too.

I wanted to tell him what was in my heart, but I didn't know how. So I spoke what was on my mind. "Gent has this rosebush he's fussed over ever since I can remember. Summer Song, it's called. I've been thinking. Maybe I'll dig it up and plant it at the cemetery by Manny and Gent's . . ." I got so choked up I couldn't go on.

"Don't you worry, Etta May. I'll help you look after it." When it came to understanding certain feelings, Quentin was smarter than anybody.

Quentin didn't say anything more. Instead, he began to sing softly.

> Sling my guitar o'er my shoulder
> Hop a freight car to Frisco.
> All I got is pocket money
> And a yearnin' in my soul.
> Hear the wheels they are a-clackin'
> As they churn along the track,
> 'Cause I got a yearnin', burnin' in my soul.
> Yes, I'm ridin', ridin', ridin' the rails,
> Ridin' home to my honey . . .

In the field beyond, a band of crickets strummed their wings.